"This Would Be A Big Mistake," Travis Said, His Gaze Shifting From Her Eyes To Her Mouth And Back Again.

"It doesn't feel that way," Lisa told him.

"It will tomorrow." And if he had one active brain cell, he'd break this off and walk away now. While he could.

She turned her face into his palm, then looked at him again. "All my life I've worried about and planned for tomorrow. For once I'd just like to claim today and let tomorrow take care of itself."

An invitation? It was one he couldn't refuse, even if he wanted to.

Pulling her closer, Travis bent his head. His gaze locked with hers, he moved in slowly, deliberately, giving her time to change her mind. Praying she wouldn't...

Dear Reader,

Summer vacation is simply a state of mind...so create your dream getaway by reading six new love stories from Silhouette Desire!

Begin your romantic holiday with *A Cowboy's Pursuit* by Anne McAllister. This MAN OF THE MONTH title is the author's 50th book and part of her CODE OF THE WEST miniseries. Then learn how a Connelly bachelor mixes business with pleasure in *And the Winner Gets...Married!* by Metsy Hingle, the sixth installment of our exciting DYNASTIES: THE CONNELLYS continuity series.

An unlikely couple swaps insults and passion in Maureen Child's *The Marine & the Debutante*—the latest of her popular BACHELOR BATTALION books. And a night of passion ignites old flames in *The Bachelor Takes a Wife* by Jackie Merritt, the final offering in TEXAS CATTLEMAN'S CLUB: THE LAST BACHELOR continuity series.

In *Single Father Seeks...* by Amy J. Fetzer, a businessman and his baby captivate a CIA agent working under cover as their nanny. And in Linda Conrad's *The Cowboy's Baby Surprise,* an amnesiac FBI agent finds an undreamed-of happily-ever-after when he's reunited with his former partner and lover.

Read these passionate, powerful and provocative new Silhouette Desire romances and enjoy a sensuous summer vacation!

Joan Marlow Golan

Joan Marlow Golan
Senior Editor, Silhouette Desire

Please address questions and book requests to:
Silhouette Reader Service
U.S.: 3010 Walden Ave., P.O. Box 1325, Buffalo, NY 14269
Canadian: P.O. Box 609, Fort Erie, Ont. L2A 5X3

The Marine &
the Debutante

MAUREEN CHILD

Published by Silhouette Books
America's Publisher of Contemporary Romance

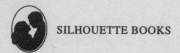

SILHOUETTE BOOKS

ISBN 0-373-76443-X

THE MARINE & THE DEBUTANTE

Visit Silhouette at www.eHarlequin.com

Printed in U.S.A.

Books by Maureen Child

MAUREEN CHILD

is a California native who loves to travel. Every chance they get, she and her husband are taking off on another research trip. The author of more than sixty books, Maureen loves a happy ending and still swears that she has the best job in the world. She lives in Southern California with her husband, two children and a golden retriever who has delusions of grandeur.

Visit her Web site at www.maureenchild.com.

This book is dedicated to the men and women
of the United States Marine Corps. Their courage
and devotion to duty allow the rest of us to enjoy
the freedom of living in the best country in the world.
Thank you all from the bottom of my heart.
Semper Fi

One

"If I get shot saving some spoiled little rich girl," Travis Hawks muttered, "finish the job and kill me."

"Deal," J.T. whispered.

Travis sent the other man a quick look. In the darkness, all he could see of his friend's face were the whites of his eyes—and his grin. Camouflage paint disguised his features, just like the other two men on the recon team.

"You agreed to that mighty damn fast," Travis said with a wry smile as he checked the load in his rifle for the third time.

"What're friends for?" he asked. "You'd do the same for me, wouldn't you?"

A slight rustle from the bushes had them both spinning around, alert and ready. Deke poked his head through, whispered, "Travis, go get the girl and let's get the hell outa here."

"Right."

"Your charges set?"

"You need to ask?" he asked, already dropping to his belly for the crawl to the squat, stone house just fifty feet from them. Hell, Travis was the best damn explosives man in the Corps and everybody here knew it. Most days, he was even better than Jeff Hunter, the Gunnery Sergeant who led their team, though Travis wasn't stupid enough to say that out loud. And when it came right down to it, his expertise was probably what had gotten them roped into this mission.

Which just went to show that pride in your work could get you into all kinds of trouble. But it wasn't time to think of things like that now. Instead he focused his concentration on the job. Flattening out on the dirt, rifle cradled in his arms, he used his elbows to drag his body across the open ground between the team and their target.

Voices drifted to him on the still night air. And though he didn't exactly speak the language, the tone told him the men guarding the woman were relaxed. Good. He hoped they stayed that way.

Sweat pooled at the base of his neck despite the near-freezing temperature. It got damn cold in the desert at night. His knees and elbows propelled him quickly to the stone house, and as he slowly came to his feet alongside the blacked-out window, he quietly released the breath he'd been holding. So far, so good.

Just as he'd expected, there were no guards posted on the perimeter. Apparently, these guys felt pretty secure. Bad for them, Travis thought, good for us.

He lifted the window sash and prayed that the intel they'd received before starting this mission had been completely accurate. If there were guards in the room with her, then all hell was about to break loose. Travis paused for a heartbeat or two, to listen. When he was convinced that it was still safe, he slipped into the darkened room, moving as quietly as combat boots allowed.

His vision already adjusted to the blackness, Travis had no problem locating the woman. She was lying on her back upon the only piece of furniture in the room—a narrow cot. Her deep, even breathing told him she was asleep. In a few steps he was beside her. Clamping one hand over her mouth to keep her quiet, he waited for her to wake up.

Instantly she did just that.

And he almost wished she hadn't.

She fought against his hold on her like a tiger coming out of her cage looking for dinner. Arms, legs, teeth joined the fight, and Travis was hard-pressed to contain her. Keeping his hand over her mouth, despite the teeth digging into his palm, he pinned her to the cot beneath his own body and muttered, "U.S. Marines. Knock it off, lady. I'm here to get you out."

She stopped fighting just as quickly as she'd started.

He stared down at the whites of her eyes and watched them narrow dangerously. Then very deliberately she reached for his wrist and yanked his hand from her mouth.

Finally, he thought. A little gratitude.

"It's about time," she snapped, and shattered his little hero fantasy.

A flash of anger shot through him, followed by a blast of sheer fear. He threw a glance at the door across the room, then looked back at the woman who was about to blow this whole damn thing.

Keeping his voice no more than a whispered threat, he ordered, "Lady, shut up and get moving."

"Fine," she said softly, already swinging her legs off the cot and standing up. "But for heaven's sake, you people took your own sweet time about getting here."

"Oh, for the love of—" He didn't even finish the oath. Didn't have time. Had to get moving before her captors took it into their heads to check on their little pot of gold. "Follow me," he said, and headed for the window and escape.

"I need my purse."

"Forget it," he muttered, peering out into the darkness before turning to help her across the sill. Stunned, he saw she hadn't followed him at all. Instead she was flat on her belly, reaching under the damn cot for her damn purse.

He stalked back across the room and grabbed her elbow. "There's no mall here. You don't need daddy's credit cards. And there's no time for this, princess," he muttered.

She yanked free of his grip, then, meeting hostility with pure venom, she said, "I've waited two weeks for you. You can wait another minute for me."

Short of hitting her over the head and dragging her ass out of there, he didn't have much choice. Through his headset, he heard a whispered question come through loud and clear. "Where the hell are you?"

Scowling, Travis touched the black band at the base of his neck, pressed the sensitive throat mike to his larynx and muttered, "Waitin' on princess. Comin' right out." He kept one eye on the closed door and mentally ticked off the seconds as they passed. There were too many of them. They were asking for trouble, he told himself. This couldn't be good. "Move it, lady."

"Got it," she said, and stood up, holding a white leather saddle bag dangling from what was probably a real gold chain. She slipped it over her head so that the chain lay across her chest and the purse settled at her hip. Then she nodded at him, and Travis grabbed her and propelled her toward the window—and freedom.

"Come on, now," he prodded. "Climb out and let's get gone."

She sat on the window ledge, gathered up her skirt and started to swing her legs through. Then she stopped. "You know," she said softly, "you could be a little nicer, here. I *am* the victim, remember?"

Travis sucked in a gulp of air. He was seriously beginning to doubt that. In fact, another few minutes of this and he was going to start feeling some real sympathy for her abductors.

He bent down, put his face just a breath away from hers and whispered, "Listen up, princess. We got about a minute and a half to get clear of this place and still have time to make the chopper pickup. Now, you want to move that pretty ass of yours before I kick it into gear?"

Her eyes widened and for a second, there, it

looked as though she might argue. Then apparently she changed her mind. Swinging her legs over the window ledge, she dropped onto the desert floor and waited for him to follow.

There was just no time to throw her to the ground and try to slink out the way he'd come in, Travis told himself. Instead he took a tight grip on her upper arm and dragged her along behind him as he made a run for cover.

Stumbling and muttering under her breath, she managed to keep up. Barely. And as soon as he hit the low clump of bushes where the others were waiting, he dropped into a crouch, pulling her down beside him, then released her.

Deke glanced at her before fastening his gaze on Travis. "Jeff's at the rendezvous point. Let's move."

"Move where?" the woman asked.

"Right behind ya," Travis muttered, ignoring her and her question.

In seconds Deke and J.T. had melted into the low-lying bushes, and Travis pushed the woman after them. "Get going," he said, then added, "and keep low."

Thankfully, she kept quiet and did as she was told. Travis threw one last look at the stone hut behind them, then moved silently off after her, guarding their escape. His mind blanked out as it always did at times like this. He did *what* he had to, *when* he had to. He didn't think. Didn't question. Just moved on instinct.

His gaze swept the landscape, back and forth, but kept drifting back to the woman in front of him. Her stupid full skirt snagged on every bush she passed. He shook his head and clenched his teeth together to keep from shouting at her to hurry up. Already the others were too far ahead of them. She was slowing everything down.

"Damn it," he muttered under his breath. "Can't you move any faster?"

Lisa Chambers stopped dead and glared at him over her shoulder. She'd had just about enough. Two weeks of sitting in that cramped little hot box, surrounded by men who wore bandoliers of ammunition with the aplomb her father's friends wore cummerbunds; and now this. She was hot, tired, hungry, cranky and she'd gone *way* too long without a bath. She for darn sure wasn't going to stand for some Southern-fried Marine cursing her for walking too slowly.

Cold night air crawled over her skin, sending bone-deep shivers to every inch of her body. The gold chain across her chest chafed her neck and the solid slap of her purse against her hip was beginning to throb.

Hard to believe that in the span of a few minutes a person could experience so many different sorts of emotions. When she'd first awakened to the feel of a man's hand across her mouth, her first reaction had been sheer terror—followed, naturally, by the instinct to defend herself. For one brief, horrifying moment, she'd thought her captors had finally decided to do more than keep her isolated and afraid.

Then the very next instant, relief had crashed down on her as she'd heard that purely American voice drawl the words, "U.S. Marines." The "cavalry" had been so long in coming, she'd about given up hope.

Tears she didn't have time to shed stung her eyes, and she blinked them back with practiced ease. She hadn't shown her captors any weaknesses, and she wouldn't let her rescuer see any, either.

"You know," she said, sarcasm dripping from her words, "a little sensitivity wouldn't be out of line here."

He didn't even look at her. Well, she was pretty sure he didn't. In the moonless dark, he was almost indistinguishable from the night, so it was hard to be sure. Unlike her. In her sunny-yellow dress, she probably stood out like a spotlight on an empty stage. And that thought gave her a cold chill deep enough to have Lisa give the surrounding darkness a quick, wary look. When she turned back toward him, she saw the whites of his eyes narrow dangerously at her.

"Lady," he said and his slow, menacing Southern drawl drifted in the air, "you want sensitivity, call the Navy. You want help, call the Marines." Then he dropped to one knee and pulled something from under the closest bush. Flicking her another quick glance, he ordered, "Get a move on, darlin'."

"Darlin'?" she repeated, but her voice was lost in the blast of a nearby explosive.

Lisa gasped and staggered back a step or two. Her gaze locked on a fireball that roared up as if thrown from the bowels of hell by a demon bent on destruction. Light showered down on them and the area, but before she could do much more than notice that the Marine was running at her, he had hold of her arm and she was moving, too.

His hand made one warm spot on her body, but his grip was anything but tender. The fabric of her skirt caught, then ripped free as he half dragged, half pushed her along the path. Her high heels sank into the sand as if the desert itself was trying to hold her back. The delicate pumps were perfect for a day of shopping or even a night of dancing. But they weren't exactly prime jogging equipment. Her feet ached, her head was pounding, and she wondered absently if she would survive her rescue. Her "hero" stayed just a step behind her, obviously guarding her back, but she almost wished he was in front of her so she'd know where to go. She had no idea. Only knew that she wanted out of this place. Now.

She wanted to be back in the States. Back at her father's house. In that glorious, sky-blue bathtub that dominated the bathroom in her suite of rooms. She wanted freshly fluffed towels, lit candles sputtering on the sea-foam colored tiles and a chilled glass of wine at her elbow. She wanted running water, hair dryers and *toilet paper*. Oh, God, please help her to get out of this mess, she prayed frantically.

"Damn it," he muttered, and she heard that curse with a sinking sigh.

"What now?" she demanded, still moving, due to his hand shoving at the small of her back. "What is it? What's wrong?"

"What isn't?" he grumbled, and stopped dead.

Lisa stopped, too, waiting for him. He might be irritating, but as far as she was concerned, he was the rescuer and she was going to stick to him like glue.

"Keep going," he shouted, the need for silence apparently lost with the first blast.

"Where?" she demanded, not moving another step.

"Son of a—" His voice broke off and he pulled another something out from yet another bush, and this time she was close enough to watch him. His fingers moved surely, efficiently. He flipped up a small, clear-plastic dome, flicked a silver switch and then moved his thumb to a bright-green glowing button. He punched it, and another blast rocked the desert night.

This one was closer and Lisa stared at it, awestruck by the fierce beauty of it. But beneath the roar of the explosion, she heard shouts. Angry shouts.

And she knew her captors were chasing them.

"This can't be good."

"Darlin', none of this is good," he muttered, jumping to his feet and grabbing her hand. "Let's get the lead out, huh?"

They ran.

And ran.

And when she thought she'd drop, when she was wishing she could take her aching legs off and throw them away, they ran some more.

"Runnin' late. Not gonna make it," he said, more to himself than to her.

She swallowed hard, fought for breath and still managed to ask, "You mean the helicopter?"

"Damn straight."

"We have to make it."

He threw her a worried look. "The extraction point's up ahead."

Extraction? Sounded like a dental visit, which would have been more fun than this.

From far off she heard the dull slap of a helicopter's blades whipping the air. Her heartbeat thundered in her chest. Close, she thought. So close. They'd make it. They had to make it.

Every step was a trial.

Every breath a victory.

Behind them she heard voices. Shouts. And the occasional gunshot. Lisa winced and instinctively ducked her head as they ran forward. The wash from the chopper blades pushed at them. In the indistinct light she saw other men—two, then three—sprinting for the helicopter. A Marine stood in the open door, an automatic weapon in his hand, spitting gunfire, covering their escape.

Then that Marine crumpled as if he'd been a puppet and someone had cut his strings. A moment later she heard a rifle shot, followed by several more in quick succession.

"Get down, damn it!" the man behind her said, crouching and pulling her down with him.

"Why are we waiting?" she demanded, looking up at him, trying to read his expression through the camouflage war paint he wore.

"We won't make it," he said tightly. "Too much open ground. They'll pick us off."

"We—we *have* to make it," she said, shifting her

gaze back to the helicopter where another Marine had taken the place of the first one. He fired quick, staccato bursts from his weapon, and flashes of fire erupted from the barrel of his gun.

"Can't."

"No." She couldn't go back to that place. To being a prisoner. She wouldn't. Lisa half stood, determined to make a run for the only way out.

But she didn't get a step.

He yanked her back down with such force, her butt slammed into the ground. His grip on her upper arm tightened and he pulled her around to face him.

"We can't make it. And if they sit here much longer waitin' on us, they won't get out, either."

Panic reared its ugly head. He couldn't mean what she thought he meant. "What are you saying?"

He didn't bother to explain. Instead he stood up briefly, hitched his rifle high over his head and waved it in some sort of silent signal.

"No," she said, hoping he hadn't done what she thought he had. "Don't do that!"

"Come on," he said tightly, dragging her off to the right, deeper into the shadows.

Lisa looked back as the helicopter lifted off, taking her only means of escape with it.

Two

Travis kept a tight hold on the woman's hand and ran for it. He could only hope that their pursuers were still far enough away that some fast running and clever hiding would do the trick. If they could get gone quick enough, the men still firing rifles at a now-disappearing chopper, would assume that their prey had escaped in that helicopter. *If* he could get the woman stumbling along behind him to shut up and move. As he'd already learned, that was no easy task.

"Are you out of your mind?" she demanded.

He had to give her credit. Even in her fury, she

kept her voice low enough that it wouldn't carry across the desert.

"It's been said," he agreed, darting a quick look back over his shoulder. No pursuit yet. Good. Keep moving, he told himself.

"You waved them off," she continued, stunned disbelief coloring her voice. "I *saw* you. The helicopter was there. They were waiting for us. Our only escape and you waved them off!"

He shot her a glare that would have terrified a lesser woman. Naturally, it didn't have the slightest effect on the one woman he wanted it to.

"You're insane," she muttered.

"I'm startin' to agree with you," he snapped. Who else but a crazy man would volunteer for such a mission? He could have been on leave back home. Of course, then his sisters would have been ragging on him. But at least *they* were family. "Now shut the hell up and follow me."

"Like I have a choice," she managed to say breathlessly.

They kept going, and one part of Travis's mind gave quiet thanks for the terrain. This wasn't the kind of desert that you found out in the middle of the Mojave. The *real* desert was farther out. This area was more like the landscape that he grew up with back in Texas. Sand, sure, but more rocky. With clumps of bushes and a few sparse but hardy trees. A ring of low-lying hills, which probably passed for mountains around here, surrounded them, and he was hoping to find refuge there.

The darkness was their friend.

They could lose themselves in the night and hopefully, before dawn, they'd be huddled in a cave somewhere and he'd have a chance to think of alternate escape plans. While he ran, making sure the princess was keeping up with him, his mind worked the problem. He had water. And rations. And a radio and weapons. He could do this. *They* could do this.

It was just going to take some creativity. Adapting and overcoming. Hell, he'd been trained for just this sort of thing. And damned if he wasn't going to pull it off.

"Come on," he urged quietly. "Just keep moving and everything'll work out."

"Like it has so far?" she wondered aloud.

He threw one look at the star-studded sky and silently asked, Why me? And more important, Why her? This would have been a helluva lot easier if he'd just been asked to rescue a reasonable person. But this woman had been trouble from the get-go, and he suspected that it wasn't going to get much better.

They walked for hours, until Lisa was ready to throw dignity to the wind and beg the guy in charge of this little forced march for a rest. But she doubted he would even hear her. Long accustomed to the darkness, she had no trouble seeing him clearly. Tall and rangy, he moved effortlessly across the rocky ground. He never seemed to get tired. He never let go of her hand, and his gaze continually scanned their surroundings, constantly on alert. His profile was sharp, dangerous looking, without an ounce of softness in it. The camouflage paint only made him look scarier—more remote. His jaw was hard and square and his nose had obviously been broken at least once…. Her sympathies were entirely with the break*er* not the break*ee*. She hadn't had a good look at his eyes yet, but she had the distinct feeling they'd be all business, no matter the color.

Well, if she had to be stranded in the middle of nothing, she told herself, it was better to be with a man so clearly equipped to handle it. A stray notion shot through her mind and she laughed shortly at the thought of her last fiancé trying to survive out here. James hadn't been able to hail a cab in Manhattan successfully.

"Was that a laugh?" he asked, slowing his steps.

Grateful, Lisa slowed down, too, and instantly felt her calf muscles cramp. She winced, nodded and admitted, "Yes, I laughed. Maybe I'm hysterical."

"Swell."

She looked up at him. Darn him, anyway, he

wasn't even winded. "I'm kidding," she said, then added, "I think."

Releasing her hand, he gave her a long, thoughtful look, swung his pack to the ground and said, "Sit for a few minutes. Take a breather."

"Oh, thank heaven," she muttered, and dropped like a stone. Then she had to shift slightly to inch *off* the stone she'd landed on. Perfect. Well, why shouldn't her behind ache as much as every other spot on her body?

"Here," he said, handing her a beige, flask-shaped canteen. "Have a drink. Not much, though. I've only got two and they've got to last us."

Lisa nodded, too tired to argue, which was saying something, she supposed. Unscrewing the cap, she lifted the canteen and took one big mouthful of warm, wet, wonderful water. Then she swallowed, letting the liquid slide down her throat like a blessing, before handing the canteen back. She hadn't even realized just how thirsty she was. And right now, the metallic-flavored water tasted better than the finest bottle of wine.

Now that they'd stopped running, the cold night air had caught up with her. She shivered and clapped her hands to her upper arms, rubbing them up and down, trying to create some warmth. Funny how running and being terrified will keep you all toasty.

"Cold?"

She nodded.

He shrugged the small pack off his back and swung it to the ground. Then, setting his gun to one side, he quickly undid the buttons on his sand-colored uniform shirt and pulled it off, revealing a Marine-green T-shirt that looked as though it had been molded to his brawny chest.

"You don't have to do that," she said, both grateful and embarrassed to be taking the shirt off his back.

"Just put it on, princess."

Well, so much for gratitude. She snatched the shirt out of his hands and shoved her arms into the long sleeves. The cuffs hung well past her wrists, to flop over the edge of her fingertips. But it was warm—the fabric still held a touch of his body heat along with his scent.

He stood up again, grabbed his rifle and gave another quick look around.

She looked down to see the mammoth shirt hanging to nearly the hem of her dress. Oh, if her friends could see her now. Lisa Chambers, girl fashion plate, dressed as a miniature soldier. But she was warm and that was saying a lot.

"I, uh…" Gratitude came hard, considering that he wasn't one of her favorite people at the moment.

"Forget it." He cut her off, clearly not interested

in thanks. "Now, you stay put," he said. "I'll be right back."

"What?" Panic reared up inside her, and she shot a wild look around her at the surrounding darkness. *Anything* or *anyone* could be hiding out there. "You're leaving me here? Alone?"

He shot her a grin. "Gonna miss me?"

Her stomach flip-flopped. Amazing what an effect that smile could have on an exhausted, thirsty, hungry, obviously delusional woman.

"Don't worry about it," he said, before she could come up with a witty reply. "I'm just goin' back to make sure I've covered our tracks well enough."

"I didn't realize you *had* been covering our tracks," she said, looking back over her shoulder as if she could actually see into the darkness and the trail he'd been working to erase.

"That's my job," he said, already moving off into the shadows.

"Who are you, anyway?" she demanded. "Daniel Boone?"

He glanced back at her and gave her another one of those grins. "Nah, the name's Travis Hawks, ma'am. But I appreciate the compliment."

"Well, my name's Lisa Chambers," she retorted as he disappeared into the darkness. Her voice dropped to a whisper as she added, "It's *not* 'ma'am.'"

What felt like hours but what was probably only a few minutes, passed, and she heard him approaching. At least, she *hoped* it was Travis Hawks.

It was.

She released a breath she hadn't realized she'd been holding as he moved to her side. Then she noted he wasn't even breathing heavily.

Tipping her head back, she looked up at him. "Aren't you even tired?" she asked, disgusted that he showed no signs of the fatigue swamping her.

He spared her a quick glance, then lifted his gaze back to the wild, arid landscape. "I'll be tired when we get where we're goin'."

"Well," she said, "I had no idea I was in the company of a superhero." Muffling a groan, Lisa pulled her right foot onto her left knee and massaged the tight knot in her calf. "And where *is* 'where we're goin',' exactly?" she asked, mocking his drawl.

"There," he said, ignoring her gibe as he pointed to a low range of mountains.

She squinted into the distance and felt her heart drop to the pit of her stomach. "You're kidding," she said, "right?"

"No, ma'am."

"Lisa," she reminded him, "not 'ma'am.' And that's probably another five miles," she protested, already thinking about the extra aches and pains headed her way.

He reached into the inside pocket of his shirt and pulled out a fabric-covered map. He studied it for a few minutes, then shifted his gaze back to her. "More like three."

"Well, heck," she said, sarcasm dripping from her words. "That's different, then. What're we waiting for?"

Folding the map and tucking it away again, he dropped to one knee beside her and reached for her leg.

"Hey!" She stiffened and tried to pull away, but let's face it, she was so tired a snail could have overtaken her. Let alone Mr. I'll-Get-Tired-Later.

"Relax, princess," he said, his fingers kneading the tight flesh. "I'm just tryin' to help."

She muffled a yelp and told herself to stop him. She shouldn't be letting him do this. She hated him. She hated what he was forcing her to do. Heck, she'd walked more today than she usually did in a month of treadmill exercising. And it was all *his* fault. If he hadn't waved off that helicopter, she'd be winging her way toward an American Embassy somewhere, already anticipating a hot bath and a good meal and some fresh clothes. So, yeah. She hated him and she should be telling him all this while at the same time making him stop massaging her legs. And yet…it felt so *good*. Pain shimmered inside her, blossomed, then disappeared under the wash of warmth drawn from his fingertips.

He moved from one calf to the other, his strong fingers easing away the tightness in her muscles until she almost wanted to weep with the pleasure of it all. Okay, she thought. Maybe he's not so bad. Maybe he's doing the best he can. Maybe he's sorry that he's working her so hard. Maybe…

"Okay, that's it," he announced. "Let's get movin'." He dropped her leg as if it were a seashell; picked up, examined, then discarded as useless.

And just like that she hated him again.

"That's your idea of a 'rest'?" she asked. "Three whole minutes?"

Standing up, he held one hand out to her and pulled her to her feet. "Sun'll be up in a few hours," he said sagely, his gaze drifting across the far horizon. "I want to be tucked away nice and quiet before that happens."

She shifted her gaze to the same horizon and realized that the sky did look just a bit brighter. They'd been walking all night. No wonder she was tired, for pity's sake.

"And you think I'm going to be able to walk three more miles in under three hours?" If the way she was feeling at the moment was any indication, she'd be lying in a crumpled heap inside of a half hour. Her own fallen image rose up in her brain, and Lisa imagined the headlines—Billionaire's Daughter Found Dead in Desert. And, of course, there'd be pictures. Of her mummified body wearing her once fashionable, now pitiful, designer dress.

Now there's an epitaph.

"You'll make it," he said, his words shattering the thoughts in her mind with the steely ring of determination in his tone.

She looked up at him. Funny, she hadn't noticed until just this minute how tall he was. At least six-three. At five-nine, Lisa was no munchkin, but he made her feel tiny in comparison. Maybe she could make it. With his help. He didn't seem the kind of man to give up easily. If he had, they would have been captured hours ago.

"Okay, general," she said, bravely swallowing the knot of fear lodged in her throat. "You lead, I'll follow."

"Ooh-rah," he said, and gave her a smile that nearly knocked her over.

"Ya-hoo," she answered, hoping she'd see that smile again really soon.

Travis wouldn't have admitted it under torture, but he was beat, down to the ground. The cold was keeping him awake for now, but if he didn't get some sleep soon, neither one of them was going to get out of here. Which was why he nearly shouted in joy when he spotted the cave.

If he hadn't been looking specifically for just this, he never would have noticed it. A slight overhang of rock jutted out from the side of the mountain, looking like nothing more than an extrawide crevice. Yet, on closer inspection, he found a narrow but deep cave that would be a perfect place to hide.

Every bone in his body cried out for rest, but before he could, he had to make sure the place was safe. Leaving the princess at the mouth of the cave, he took his rifle and snatched a chem light out of his equipment belt. Cracking the hard plastic case, he then shook it until the crystals inside glowed a soft green. An ordinary flashlight or a flare would be too bright in this all-encompassing blackness. Too easy to spot from a distance. This thing would give off enough light to see by and still be hard to spot by their enemies. Carefully he inspected the shelter. The eerie green light glowed and cast soft, indistinct shadows on the rock walls. His right hand gripping the rifle, he held the light up high in his left as he squinted into the darkness.

"What do you see?"

He winced as her voice seemed to echo in the stony enclosure, and he hoped to hell the place was as empty as it seemed.

"Quiet." His voice was hardly more than a raspy

hush of sound. And still it traveled back to her with no problem.

"And what does quiet look like?" she muttered.

Travis grinned reluctantly and shook his head. This damn woman was as stubborn as he was. A moment later, though, the smile on his face faded as he concentrated on the task at hand. The walls were solid, no holes where critters could crawl or slither through from somewhere else. There was no sign of human habitation in here, but there was always the threat of snakes. Growing up in Texas had given him a healthy respect for the reptiles, and he sure as hell didn't want any surprises while they slept.

Damn, his eyes felt heavy. Gritty. As though he hadn't slept in a year. He blinked, shook his head again and focused. As he did, a slight movement caught the corner of his eye, and he turned his head to follow the snake's movement. Just one, it was moving fast across the sandy ground.

"Damn it," he whispered, knowing he couldn't risk a gunshot to kill it. He'd been prepared to fire on a hostile human, but he'd rather not risk a rifle shot being heard for miles for the sake of killing a snake. Gritting his teeth, Travis set his rifle down, grabbed his knife and killed it, neatly slicing its head from its body.

Then he stood and gave a last look around. Everything else was secure. If the snake had had friends, they were long gone. The cave wasn't much, but it looked damn good to him at the moment. They were safe—for now. They could get some rest and hide until he figured out the best route to get out of this country.

"What's going on back there?" she called, and he heard the fear in her voice.

That woman could drive a saint right out of heaven, he thought. But then, a part of him couldn't really blame her for being scared. She'd already been through more than most folks would face in a lifetime, and to give her her due, she hadn't folded. And Travis admired grit in a person, male or female.

Of course, that didn't mean he didn't wish she was anywhere but there. But wishes wouldn't do a damn bit of good. They were stuck together. And the fact that she was too blasted good-looking for comfort shouldn't come into it. She was his responsibility—nothing else. He'd best remember that. "It's okay," he said. "You can come in now."

"Good," she said, and her voice told him how quickly she was making her way down the length of the cave. "I was getting worried back there by myself. You know you could have left me one of your little Halloween pumpkin light thingies."

"It's a chem light. Not the kind used in pumpkins."

"Whatever," she said, and he watched her walk into the circle of soft-green light. "The point is, it's really dark in here and I—"

Her voice broke off as her gaze fastened on the dead snake. She took several deep breaths, slapped one hand to her chest and said, "Oh, God."

"It's dead."

"That's supposed to make me feel better?" Eyes wide, she backed up and looked around frantically as if expecting to see a pack of snakes sneaking up on her flank.

He bent down, picked up the carcass and held it up admiringly. At least a three-footer. "You'll think better of it once it's cooked."

"Cooked?"

Travis could have sworn he heard her gag.

"Waste not, want not," he told her.

"Look before you leap," she countered.

"He who hesitates is lost," he said, figuring this could go on awhile.

"He who eats snake will get sick," she told him.

"That's not an old saying."

"It's one of my favorites," she said. "As of right now."

Travis laughed shortly and set his pack down, then laid the snake alongside it. Jamming the end of the light into the sand at his feet, he said, "Have a seat. I'm going out to gather some brush. We can make a small fire.''

''You're leaving me here?'' she asked, lifting one hand to point at the snake. ''With *that?*''

''Trust me,'' he said tightly, ''*you're* more dangerous than he is.''

She swung her hair back from her eyes, and in the green glow those blue eyes gleamed like sapphires. Her face pale, her features drawn with fatigue and fear, she was still pretty enough to take a man's breath away.

And he realized he'd been right.

She *was* dangerous.

Three

An hour later they were crouched beside a fire so tiny it hardly qualified as flames. But still, the hiss and snap of the burning brush was…comforting, somehow. Except of course, for the snake meat sizzling on a stick.

Lisa cringed just a little and shifted her gaze from the fire to the man opposite her. She watched as he used a rag from his pack to wipe the camouflage paint off his face. With steady, long strokes, he slowly revealed more of his features. Jet-black eyebrows. And his eyes. Darned if they didn't look like melted chocolate—rich and dark—and they had almost precisely the same effect on her. A twinge of hunger, mixed with expectation. In the weird green light, his features looked sharp. Resolute. His nose had character, she decided, and combined with that strong, square jaw, he probably could have made a fortune as a model. Instead, he made his living by dragging women across dark deserts while crazy people shot at them.

"We'll stay here until dark," Travis was saying. "Then I figure we'll head for El Bahar. It's not far and the king there is friendly to the U.S."

"Uh-huh," she said, and though she heard the snap in her tone, she couldn't seem to stop it. "And how far away is this place?"

He pulled out his map, checked it for what had to be the tenth time in the past hour, then glanced at her briefly. "Not far."

"How far?"

"A day or so," he said, deliberately ignoring the sarcasm in her voice. "But once we're in their territory, you'll be safe."

"Day *or so?*" She tried to keep the groan out of her voice but she was pretty sure she hadn't succeeded. Then, rather than concentrate on the march ahead, she focused on the last word he'd said.

Safe.

For the past two weeks of captivity, that was a word she'd concentrated on often. Before being snatched from her spur-of-the-moment shopping trip, Lisa'd never realized just how much she took her own safety for granted. It wasn't something you normally thought about. It just...*was.*

She doubted she'd ever be that complacent again. In fact, she'd probably be looking over her shoulder for years.

But she hadn't let her captors know she was scared, and she refused to give in to fear now.

"Once we're in El Bahar," he was saying, "we'll go directly to the American Embassy and call for a ride home."

"My father can send his jet."

One black eyebrow lifted, and he shook his head, chuckling wryly under his breath.

She had the distinct feeling he wasn't laughing *with* her. Stiffly she asked, "What's so funny?"

"You," he said, reaching to rotate his stick of snake meat in the fire. "A regular plane ride's just not good enough, huh? Have to call for a private jet."

All right, maybe that *had* sounded a little snooty. "I only meant—"

"Relax, princess," he said, interrupting her neatly. "I know just what you meant."

"Really."

Shifting position, Lisa folded her legs in the most ladylike manner she could manage. Wincing slightly at the movement, she tucked her torn, dirty dress down over them and shrugged out of his shirt. With the rock walls cutting off the wind, and the tiny fire, she'd finally warmed up again.

"Yes, really," Travis said, shaking his head again and leaning back against the cool rock wall. He had her number. Had had it from the moment she'd opened her eyes and looked up at him back there at the shack. And he didn't mind telling her so. "I've known women like you most of my life," he said. "The rich girls, counting out daddy's money and buying what they could never earn."

"Now just a darn minute." Her eyes flashed, outrage obvious in her tone.

"Struck a nerve, huh?" he asked, and without waiting for an answer, he went on. "Let's just look at your story so far. You decide to visit an area rife with civil unrest to do some *shopping* and promptly get snatched."

"The papers at home didn't say anything about the dangers of—"

"And then," he said, his voice easily overriding hers, "when you're in trouble up to your pretty neck, you just expect Daddy to pay the demanded ransom."

"Why wouldn't he?" she asked. "I'm his only child."

"For which he's probably grateful," Travis com-mented and took real pleasure in the murder he saw glinting in her eyes. "My point is, even if he'd paid the ransom, there was no guarantee you'd be released."

"Of course they'd have released me. Why wouldn't they?"

"Darlin'," he said, "after spending most of the day with you, I'm only surprised they didn't offer to pay your dad to take you off their hands."

"You have no right to say such—"

He waved off her indignation. "But back to our story. See, this is where me and my friends came in. The government convinced your daddy to hold off on paying up and to send us in instead."

"It's your job, isn't it?"

"My *job* is to help people who need it. Even spoiled little rich girls whose only job is to look gorgeous and spend cash that isn't theirs."

And she was gorgeous, he admitted silently, his gaze moving over her quickly, thoroughly. Even after all she'd been through, she looked damn good. Blond hair that just dusted across her shoulders was tucked behind her ears now, and a soft fringe of bangs stopped just above her finely arched eyebrows. In the firelight her eyes looked as blue as the sea at dusk, and her mouth looked delicious. Her teeth continually tugged at her bottom lip until it was all Travis could do to keep from offering to help with that little chore. Damn, this was not the time or the place or hell...*the woman* to be having these thoughts about.

He'd do well to remember that she was nothing more than a mission gone wrong. If she hadn't held him up. If she hadn't wasted so much time looking for her damn purse. If those expensive but worthless high heels had made better time in the sand...if any of those things had been different, he would already be rid of her. They'd have parted ways and he never would have had the time or opportunity to notice that her right breast was just a little fuller than her left.

Oh, man. Travis got a grip on the suddenly rampaging hormones charging through his bloodstream and reminded himself that she was no different from the girls back home. Those girls, backed by their daddies' oil money, had run roughshod over anybody in their way. And when it came to guys like him—they were happy enough to snuggle up in the dark, but they never brought his kind home to daddy.

Travis Hawks didn't come from money and as far as he could tell, having it hadn't done those girls— or this one, for that matter—any good.

"I resent that."

He blinked and drew himself back to the conversation at hand. Hell, fighting with her was one sure way to keep his mind on the job rather than on fantasies that didn't stand a snowball's chance in hell of coming true. "I bet you do," he said. "But you're not denying it."

"I do deny it," she said hotly, and leaned toward him. Firelight mirrored in her eyes until it looked as though her gaze was shooting sparks at him. "I am *not* spoiled. And for your information, I'm on the boards of some very worthwhile charities. I *do* work."

He nodded sagely, but there was amusement in his eyes. "Oh, I'm sure your telephone dialing finger gets a real workout."

That blond eyebrow lifted again and disappeared behind her bangs.

"So you work," he said. "Do you have to live off what you make? I don't think so."

"I see. Because I don't have to worry about income, what I do is worth nothing?"

"I didn't say that."

"You most certainly did."

All right, maybe he shouldn't have started any of this. It was none of his business how she lived. His job was simply to return her to the lap of luxury and get the hell out of Dodge. They had another few days together, and there was no sense in being outright enemies, for Pete's sake.

"You know what you are?" she asked, tilting her

head to one side and studying him as if he were smeared on a glass slide beneath a microscope.

"I'll bet you're about to tell me."

"I'd be happy to," she said, a soft smile curving that luscious mouth of hers.

She looked like a woman with a point to make, and Travis, like any other sane man, battened down the hatches and waited for the blow.

"You're a snob."

A short, sharp laugh shot from his throat, ricocheting off the rock walls to echo mockingly.

"A *snob?*" he repeated.

"That's right."

"Honey," he said, "I don't make enough money to be a snob."

"That's just it," she countered, folding her arms beneath her breasts and nodding at him. "You're a reverse snob."

"Oh, this should be good," he said, intrigued in spite of himself. He watched her with interest and couldn't help noticing again just how damn fine she looked, sitting there all smug in her dirty designer dress.

"Because you don't have money, you're prejudiced against those who do."

"Darlin'," he reminded her, "*you* don't have money. Your daddy does."

Her eyes narrowed, and he had the distinct feeling

that if she could have reached him, she just might have slapped his face. But since she couldn't, she kept talking. Which was, he thought wryly, worse than the slap would have been.

"You're a snob, and changing the subject won't alter that one fact."

"Yeah, right."

"Why else would you make assumptions about me?" she asked, drumming her fingertips against her upper arms. "You don't know me at all."

"Sure I do, princess," he drawled, letting the words slide out slowly on purpose. "I've known you most of my life."

She sniffed. "Trust me, if we'd ever met, I would remember."

"Okay, not you specifically," he continued. "But your kind."

"My *kind?*"

"Yep." His mother would be shamed to know it, but he was beginning to enjoy himself here. Nothing quite like a good argument to get your mind off your worries. And he pretty much figured that, by now, the "princess" was so mad at him, she wasn't thinking about her captors or about how small their chances of getting out of here were—or anything else for that matter except maybe taking his head off.

Oh, not that he'd started all of this because of the

kindness of his heart. No, she irritated him beyond measure. With her stylish clothes and her whining about having to run for her own life. But now that she was giving as good as she got...now that he saw that fire of temper in her eyes...damned if he wasn't having a good time.

"Oh yes," she said nodding, "that's a very cogent argument."

"Ah," he replied with a chuckle, "fifty-cent words. Trying to confuse the 'help'?"

"You're really a pain in the—"

"Now, that's not very ladylike, is it?" he asked, cutting her off just in time.

Inhaling sharply, she drew a long, deep breath into her lungs and held it. That did amazing things for her bustline, though Travis knew that if she realized he was noticing, she'd cut it out.

"I refuse to argue with you anymore."

"Can't think of a good comeback, eh?"

She shot him a glare that probably turned the rich boys she was used to into a pillar of ice. Travis wasn't impressed...or intimidated.

After a long minute or two she unfolded her arms and reached for her purse. Ignoring him completely, she flipped it open and began to rummage inside.

"You're a very annoying man," she muttered beneath her breath.

"Yeah and you're a walk in the park."

Her head snapped up and she gave him another one of those "mistress to half-wit servant" looks.

"I'm so happy I can amuse you," she said wryly. "You know, you may be used to this sort of thing, but I'm not."

"I can see that."

"And," she continued, keeping her hands fisted inside her purse while she looked up at him, "I don't appreciate being harassed by the man who was sent here to save me."

"And I don't appreciate listening to you complain, when it was your fault we missed the ride."

"You waved the helicopter off."

He leaned in close, locking his gaze with hers. "One man had already gone down. I waved 'em off so everyone else wouldn't die while they waited on us."

"That's not fair."

"But accurate."

She inhaled sharply, let it out again, then asked, "That man. Do you think he's…"

Travis closed his mind to that thought. He didn't know who'd been standing in the open doorway of the chopper. But whoever he was, he was a fellow Marine, and Travis sure as hell didn't want to think the man had been killed because Travis hadn't been able to move the princess along any faster.

"I don't know." He narrowed his gaze at her. "But one man hurt was enough, don't you think?"

Her lips flattened into a thin line, and her eyes glimmered with what he thought might be tears. But he couldn't be sure, and in an instant that softness was gone again.

"Fine," she conceded. "It was my fault. Forgive me for not wearing my sneakers and jeans. But I didn't expect to be kidnapped and held for ransom. If I'd known I was going to have to make a desert trek…"

"You wouldn't have done a damn thing different."

She straightened her shoulders and lifted her chin. Swinging her hair back out of her face, she asked, "You really don't like me very much, do you?"

A spurt of irritation shot through him. And that irritation was aimed at both her and himself. She'd been right about one thing, anyway. He *didn't* have the right to judge her. She was his mission, pure and simple. And beyond that, there was nothing. With that thought in mind, he said, "I'll tell you what, princess. Four of us, my friends and I, came into this little hellhole to pull your pretty butt out of trouble." He leaned in toward her again, mindful of the fire. "We raced across the desert, laid down cover fire, risked a chopper pilot and his crew—got one man wounded, maybe worse—and not once…not once, since the moment you opened your eyes to look into mine, have you even said, *Thank you.*''

Even in the firelight, he saw the flush that stained her pale, smooth skin, and Travis knew he'd hit his mark. For all the good it did him.

Then, even more irritated that he'd said too much, he picked up the stick, pulled it away from the fire and gingerly tested the snake meat with two fingers. Glancing at her, he said, ''It's done.''

''Uh-huh.'' She wasn't convinced.

''You'll like it.''

''Let me guess,'' she said. ''Tastes just like chicken.''

''Pretty much,'' he agreed.

''I'll never know for sure,'' Lisa said, watching the skewered meat as if half expecting it to still be able to strike. ''No way am I going to eat a snake.''

''We both need to eat,'' he said, his tone deliberately patient. ''And believe me when I say that this snake tastes better than a tuna-casserole MRE.''

Confusion shone in her eyes before she warily asked, ''Okay, I admit it. I have to know. What exactly is an MRE?''

''Meals ready to eat,'' he said shortly, and pulled a thick, green plastic, rectangular package from his pack. Stabbing the end of the shish kebab stick into the dirt, he ripped open the plastic and pulled out a flat, brown-cardboard box. He held it out to her. Stamped on one end, were the words Tuna Casserole.

"Good Lord," she said, looking from the box to his dark brown eyes. "They expect you to eat something that comes packaged like that?"

"Yep," he said with a shrug, then added, "and it's not half-bad, either. But the snake'll be better."

"No thanks."

His features tightened briefly. "Up to you, but you'll be almighty hungry before too long."

Lisa smiled and pulled her hands free of her purse. Travis's gaze dropped to what she held. Two big chunks of bread.

"You have food in there?" he asked, surprised.

"Why else would I need my purse?" she retorted. "Like you said, there aren't many malls out here."

Travis winced slightly as he felt his own words coming back to bite him in the ass. "Where'd you get it?" he asked softly.

She shrugged and began to pull more food out of that saddlebag of hers. Pieces of dried meat, parts of oranges, a handful of dates. "Every time they fed me, I hid half of whatever it was. Then, when they forgot to feed me, I'd at least have something." She shrugged as if it didn't matter, and that shrug hit him hard.

"You hid part of your food," he repeated, looking at her with a new admiration. And damn it, respect filled him, too. She'd survived. It probably hadn't been easy, either. He would have figured that a woman like her would collapse under the conditions she'd been living in. But she'd not only stood up to them, she'd come out on top. She'd done what she had to do to survive. She'd used her head, protecting herself, looking out for the future. Not many people would have been smart—or strong enough to keep back extra food just in case.

The princess had just gone up several notches in his estimation.

"It only made sense," she said, obviously trying to make light of what she'd done. "After all, who knew if they'd get tired of feeding a spoiled little rich girl. I thought it would be smart to store some food…just in case."

Travis nodded thoughtfully and met her gaze. "It *was* smart. Damn smart. Most people would have eaten when they were hungry, not thinking about tomorrow."

She smiled then, and something inside Travis's chest lurched hard against his rib cage. Much to his own surprise, he realized it was his heart.

"Would you like some bread to go along with your snake?" she asked, holding out a chunk of flat bread toward him.

"Yeah, princess—*Lisa*," he corrected. "I believe I would. Thanks."

Her fingers brushed across his skin and Travis tried not to think about the warmth blasting its way through his veins at her slightest touch. Then her gaze locked with his, and she very clearly said, "No, Travis. Thank *you*."

And staring into those sea-blue eyes of hers, he knew a bridge had sprung up between them.

It might be a little shaky...but it was there.

Four

_____

With the words she should have said hours ago, something indefinable changed between them. Lisa felt it. And she knew he did, too. She pulled her hand back and tried not to notice the tingling in her fingertips. But it was as if she'd touched a live electrical wire rather than the callused palm of a man's hand. Her skin hummed with an energy she'd never felt before, and she wasn't at all sure what to do about it.

This possibility had never occurred to her.

She'd never counted on such an instant, overpowering attraction.

Especially to a man who was so completely the opposite of what she'd always thought of as "her type."

Lisa would be the first to admit that she hadn't shown great judgment in the past. After all, you couldn't make and break five engagements and not start doubting your ability to choose wisely.

Her string of fiancés proved that much. A doctor, a lawyer, an investment banker, a college professor and a stock broker. The closest she'd ever come to the "wild side" was her professor. He taught parapsychology and though it was weird, he *was* a professor. And though none of them had worked out, they had at least made sense.

This thrumming, pulse pounding, dry mouth response to a man she hardly knew did not.

But knowing that didn't change a thing.

The men in her past had been professionals. They were a part of her world. She understood them in a way she would never be able to understand this man with the serious Daniel Boone fixation.

And it didn't seem to matter.

Something flashed in Travis's chocolate eyes, and Lisa sucked in a quiet breath. Something hot and liquid settled low in the pit of her stomach and sent out tentacles of awareness that reached every corner of her body. Wow. If just touching his hand could do that to her, she wondered what a kiss would be like.

Her gaze locked on his mouth and her insides trembled. Oh, this probably wasn't a good idea. She had who-knew-how-many days left to be in his company and he'd already made it pretty clear what he thought of her. So there was no way this was going anywhere. Still, she thought as her gaze lifted to meet his, a private little fantasy or two couldn't do any harm, could it?

"What's running around inside that head of yours?" he asked suddenly.

Lisa flinched guiltily, as if he could read her mind and see for himself the direction her thoughts had been taking. And the idea of that was simply too embarrassing to contemplate. So she had to think quickly to come up with something to tell him.

"Uh…" she stalled for a moment, then blurted, "I was just wondering what smells so bad…the cave, the snake or the fire." Brilliant, Lisa, she thought on a silent groan. Just brilliant.

But he accepted her statement at face value, for which she was grateful. "It's the fire," he said. "Actually, it's the brush we're usin' for fuel. Now, if we were back in Texas…" he paused and a soft smile creased his harsh features. "I'd toss some mesquite onto those flames and you'd think you'd died and gone to heaven, on the smell alone."

"Texas, huh?" she asked. A Marine *and* a Texan. Heck, no wonder he'd been so sure of their ability to traverse the desert before sunrise. He was probably convinced he could walk on water.

And a part of her wouldn't have been surprised to see him do it.

Oh, dear. She could be in big trouble, here.

"Yep," he said, and that proud smile on his face widened, deepened.

Again that lightning-fast sizzle of awareness splintered through her bloodstream, and Lisa wondered frantically how to stop her reaction to him. This wasn't the time or the place or the *man* for these kinds of feelings.

She was sitting in a *cave* for pity's sake. In the middle of a desert. *Get a grip, Lisa,* she chanted silently, but the way her heart was thudding in her chest, she had a feeling it wasn't going to do any good.

He started talking about home, and she watched pure pleasure light his eyes as he described his family's ranch, the horses, the sunsets and so much more. He talked about his family, about the small town where he'd grown up, and with every word, he painted a picture. A faraway look softened his gaze as if he was staring at a memory so good, so cherished, it was enough to wipe away thoughts of their current situation. Lines of tension in his features eased away, and his lips curved into a smile that made her wish she could see what he obviously saw so clearly.

Lisa suddenly felt very alone, and a slender thread of envy wound through her. Plainly, he loved the home he carried in his heart. She wondered what it must be like to have a *real* home—a home where people and places were so familiar they were like a part of yourself.

Raised by her father after her mother's death when she was three, Lisa had grown up in boarding schools. And when vacation time rolled around, there was no family homestead to head for. It was Spain or Paris or Switzerland. Not that she was complaining or anything. After all, most people would have loved to see all those places.

But she'd never had the comfort of her own room. Her own private space to dream or sulk in. She'd gone from hotels to rented villas, with never a place to belong. And even thinking it made her feel guilty. So many people had real problems that hers looked trifling in comparison.

Still, a twinge of regret for things she'd never known struck a familiar chord deep within her and brought to life an old ache. But she pushed that pain down into a dark hole inside and covered it over, as she'd done all her life, with a bright smile.

"My brother'll tell you that sage makes the best

fire," Travis was saying, "but for me, it's mesquite, every time."

"Your brother?"

"One of 'em," he said with a half shrug.

Another thing to be envious of, she thought briefly. How many nights had she lain awake, hungering for a sibling to argue with, share secrets with?

"I'm an only child," she said.

His mouth quirked in a half smile. "When I was a kid, there were a lot of times I wished I could say that."

"Trust me," she said, smoothing the hem of her torn, dirty dress over her knees, "it's not all it's cracked up to be."

"Yeah, well, now that we're grown," he said, "I guess I'm glad to have 'em."

"How many brothers do you have?"

"Three," he said. "And two sisters."

"Six kids?"

"We do things in a big way in Texas."

"Apparently."

"And we all know how to cook," he said, holding the still-steaming snake meat out toward her.

She eyed it with distaste, then looked up at him. "I thought we'd settled that already."

Both black eyebrows lifted and his mouth quirked into a taunting smile. "Scared?"

"Not scared," she said with a sniff. "Discerning."

"Chicken, you mean."

Lisa shook her head. "You really think you're going to get me to try that stuff by pulling a third-grade dare?"

"Bwaack, bwaack," he said, and she had to admit he did a pretty decent imitation of a chicken.

"Oh, for heaven's sake," she muttered, reaching out to snatch a piece of the meat. Before she could change her mind or get too sick to swallow, Lisa popped it into her mouth and chewed.

After a long minute she swallowed and looked into his waiting eyes.

"Well?" he asked.

"It wasn't terrible," she admitted, unwilling to give him more than that. But blast it, the stupid snake *did* taste good. As long as she didn't remind herself exactly what she was eating.

"Want some more?" he asked, a knowing smile on his face.

She sighed and said, "You're really loving this, aren't you?"

"Yeah," he said in that slow drawl of his. "I think I am."

"Gracious in victory, I see," she said wryly.

"Princess," he said, clearly enjoying himself

now, "the only good loser is a guy who's used to losin'."

Firelight flickering on his harsh features, a steely look in those dark eyes of his, he looked to Lisa like a man who was definitely not used to losing.

At the American Embassy in El Bahar, Gunnery Sergeant Jeff Hunter snapped into the telephone. "Yes, sir. We'll wait for further instructions."

He shot an irritated look at the two other men standing nearby. J.T. and Deke both looked as itchy footed as he felt. None of them were comfortable staying here at the embassy while Travis and the Chambers woman were somewhere out in the desert. Nothing worse than standing around waiting.

And with that thought uppermost in his mind, he interrupted the Colonel on the other end of the line. "Sir, if you give us the word, my team can be back in the field inside an hour. We'll find Hawks and the woman, then call for an evac."

"Under no circumstances are you to take your team back out," Colonel Sullivan ordered. "This was supposed to be a covert mission. We can't risk sending you back in. At least, not yet."

Disgusted at the fact that politics were now running what should have remained a military operation, Jeff shook his head at the two men watching him. J.T. cursed under his breath and Deke's scowl got fierce enough to boil blood.

"Understood, sir," Jeff said, not liking this one damn bit. Another minute of "yes sirring" and he hung up, dropping the receiver into the cradle with a loud crack.

"They're not letting us go in, then?"

"No," Jeff said, glancing at Deke. "They don't want to take the chance of having this whole thing on CNN by nightfall."

"So instead," J.T. muttered, "they're hanging Travis out to dry."

"Basically." Jeff shoved one hand across the top of his head and tried to figure out where this had all gone wrong.

"What about the woman?" Deke asked. "Isn't her father rattling enough cages to get some action?"

"Mr. Chambers," Jeff told him with a narrow-eyed stare, "doesn't know what happened. Yet."

"Travis'll get her out," J.T. said. "There's not a better man for this job."

"True," Jeff said, walking to the wide window of the Ambassador's office. He stared out at the busy street below, then lifted his gaze to the desert far out in the distance. It was a hard, dangerous land out there. Good thing Travis was every bit as hard and dangerous himself.

* * *

An hour later Travis stood at the mouth of the cave, letting his gaze slide slowly across the scorched landscape. The sun shone down from a sky that looked white-hot. In the distance, waves of heat shimmered, bending the land and tricking the eye. He narrowed his gaze on the wavering lines that resembled a large pool of water. But he was no stranger to mirages. He'd seen his share of them back in Texas on blistering summer days. He knew damn well that a desperate man could be fooled into chasing water that didn't exist until it was too late and the last of his strength gave out.

Taking a tighter grip on his rifle, he shifted his gaze from the mirage to slowly scan the area. No sign of anyone out there—but that didn't necessarily mean anything. He couldn't take anything for granted. It was up to him and him alone to see that Lisa Chambers made it out.

Which meant that he was going to have to stay focused. And not on her. Travis reminded himself that hormones had no business here. Hell, he'd been doing this job for years and never once had he found himself *talking* with the mission like they were on a date or something. Disgusted with himself, he knew that one slipup here could mean recapture or worse. He didn't need to have his concentration divided. He couldn't afford to see her as anything but what she was.

His responsibility.

Oh, they didn't need to be enemies. Hell, this whole rescue thing would work a lot better if they weren't. But they didn't need to be friendly, either.

What was needed here was a cool, detached professionalism. And if that meant pulling back, being a hard-ass, then that's just what he'd have to do. Better she not like him than start giving him the kind of smile he'd just seen. How was a man supposed to keep his mind on the dangers at hand when a woman like her turned on the charm?

Nope. This'd be a damn sight easier if she went back to snarling at him. Which shouldn't be at all hard to accomplish.

Turning, he slipped back down the narrow passage until he reached the end of the cave where he'd left Lisa, waiting.

"Did you see anything?" she asked, and he heard the fear underlying the calm of her words.

"No," he said shortly. "But that doesn't mean much. Still, we should be safe enough here. We'll hole up until nightfall and then leave. It'll be cooler walking at night and easier to lose ourselves in the shadows."

She nodded, but clearly wasn't looking forward to it. He didn't blame her. Hell, no way was she used to this kind of life. Probably hadn't walked farther than the curb to hail a taxi in years. But, he thought, steeling himself against a swell of sympathy, the harder he pushed her, the sooner they'd be out of here and back where they both belonged.

Which was nowhere near each other.

"Get some sleep," he said, and kicked out the last of their tiny fire. He used the toe of his boot to stomp out the dying embers until there was nothing left of them. Motioning her back against the wall of the cave, he stretched out in front of her, placing himself between her and whatever danger might approach.

"Sleep?" she repeated. "Here?"

He turned his head to look at her and told himself not to notice the fear in her eyes. "Well now, I called the Hilton, but they were full up."

"Very funny."

"I try."

"Try harder," she told him, squirming around on the rock floor, looking for a comfortable spot—and obviously not finding one.

"Pretend you're camping." He didn't even look at her when he spoke. At the moment he didn't have the energy.

"I've never been camping."

"There's a surprise."

She muttered something he didn't quite catch, but he heard the rustle of her dress across the dirt as she settled down.

"Look, princess," he said, feeling fatigue ease up from his very bones, "we're stuck here. We can't leave now. It's too damn hot out there. We wouldn't make a mile with our water supply so low."

"Yes, but—"

"We've got a chance for some sleep, and we're gonna take it."

She glanced at the dark passage leading toward the outside world, then shifted her gaze back to him. "And what if someone comes in while you're napping? What then, fearless leader?"

Well apparently she, too, had decided to back off the whole friendship thing. Which was just as well, he told himself. It was much safer for both of them that way.

Closing his eyes, he muttered, "Trust me. The guys who kidnapped you are probably throwing a party to celebrate you being gone. If they've got any sense at all, they're not lookin' for you."

And if they were, he thought, he'd hear them long before they got close enough to snatch her again. He'd learned long ago how to sleep with one eye open. As long as she was with him, she was safe.

He'd see to it.

Five

She moaned in her sleep, and Travis went on full alert.

First things first, he glanced at the entrance to the cave and saw that no one had discovered them. They were still alone. But Lisa's pain shimmered in the air around him. Going up on one elbow, he stared down at her and scowled to himself. In the dim light, he saw her features tighten, her brow furrowing as she twisted her head from side to side. Almost frantically she whispered words he couldn't quite understand.

But he heard the fear clearly.

A cold, hard hand fisted around his heart as he watched her battling demons in her sleep. Back teeth grinding together, Travis fought with his own instinct to protect. She wouldn't welcome his comfort, he knew. Hell, they'd been at each other's throats for hours. But at the same time he couldn't just sit here and watch her torturing herself with nightmares.

"Lisa," he whispered and reached out one hand toward her. He stopped short, though, and curled his fingers into a tight fist to keep from touching her. Keep it impersonal, he told himself sternly, trying to ignore the single tear rolling down her cheek.

But seeing a strong woman cry was enough to curdle his blood. What the hell was she dreaming about? Her captors? What had they done to her? During their forced march across the desert, he'd pushed her to the edge of her limits and then beyond. But she'd stood up to it. She hadn't broken. And damned if it didn't bother him to see her in the grips of something she couldn't fight.

"Princess," he said, his voice a little louder now as he tried to reach her through whatever torments she was experiencing.

"Don't." The single word came loud and clear and for some weird reason, it made him feel better. She was strong. Probably stronger than she knew.

Even in her dreams she was fighting back. Holding on.

He opened his fisted hand and touched her upper arm gently, trying not to be distracted by the cool softness of her flesh. But that was hard to do since the moment his skin came into contact with hers, heat swelled up and boiled his blood. Damn. It was like the shock of static electricity.

He swallowed hard and muttered quietly, "It's okay, princess. You're safe."

Whether it was the sound of his voice or the touch of his hand, she instantly quieted, turning her head toward him and moving closer on the rocky ground. He stretched out again and held perfectly still as she cuddled in, dropping one arm across his chest and burrowing her head into the hollow of his shoulder.

One corner of his mind knew that she didn't have the slightest idea of what she was doing. She was simply looking for comfort, the way a child in the dark might grab at a teddy bear. But the feel of her body curled into his sparked a reaction down low in his gut and threatened to swamp all of his high-and-mighty notions of keeping his distance.

He lay awake, staring into the darkness for a long time, while she slept deeply, trustingly, in his arms.

Lisa woke with a start.

Her eyes flew open. Her heartbeat thundered in

her ears. She swallowed hard, focused on the soft pillow beneath her head and for a long, frantic moment couldn't remember where she was.

Then, as the new aches and pains began to register, it all came flooding back to her. Oh, yeah. The cave. With supermarine.

How could she have forgotten any of it? Even for a minute? Heck, every inch of her body hurt. That wild race across the desert had just about wiped her out. *And,* she'd eaten *snake,* for pity's sake, then spent hours arguing with a man whose head gave new meaning to the phrase *solid rock.*

She grimaced as she shifted position carefully, and it wasn't until that moment that she realized her "pillow" was actually Travis Hawks's shoulder.

Oh, for heaven's sake. How embarrassing was this? All she'd done was fight and argue with the man, and then the minute she falls asleep, she snuggles up close? Well, the only discreet way out of this was to slip away from him before he woke up.

And she would do just that, she told herself. In a minute. The problem was, he just felt so darn good. Strong. Solid. She listened to the steady beat of his heart and felt…*safe.* Silly, she knew, considering the fact that they were hardly out of danger.

But there it was.

Ever since appearing in that horrible little room

to rescue her, he'd put her safety first. Even now, he lay alongside her, his body between hers and the mouth of the cave. His body between her and danger.

Okay, she told herself, uncomfortable with that particular line of thought, no need to start giving him more brownie points than he'd already collected. Besides, she was already in his debt. She didn't want to have to be forced to actually *like* him, too.

But whether she wanted to or not, Lisa's mind kept spinning on the subject of Travis Hawks.

Had he slept? Or had he stayed awake and on guard?

And why, she wondered, did she care?

He'd insulted her, exhausted her and infuriated her. So why should she care? The easy answer of course was, she shouldn't. This was his job. He did this all the time. She was just the latest in his no-doubt-impressive line of rescues.

Nothing special.

Lisa frowned at that bitter pill and some of the soft glow she'd been feeling faded away. Naturally she was nothing special to him. She'd never been special to anyone. Why would he be any different?

"I can hear you thinkin'," he said, his deep voice rumbling through the cave and dancing along her spine.

"Geezz!" She jumped, slapped one hand to her chest to keep her heart from flying out of her chest and pushed away from him to sit up straight. She felt a flush of heat rush to her cheeks and was grateful for the darkness. Served her right, she thought. Indulge in a little self-pity party—think some warm, fuzzy thoughts, and get caught at it. That would teach her.

Thank heaven he couldn't read minds. She cringed and, to cover her own discomfort, she retreated into arguing with him again.

"So since you couldn't run me to death, you've decided to *scare* the life out of me?"

His gaze shot straight to hers. Even in the shadowy darkness, she felt the power of that gaze, and something inside her did a slow flip.

Oh, boy.

"Not till we get where we're goin'," he said.

Figures that Captain America would come out of a deep sleep ready to march. "I take it we're leaving?"

"If it's dark enough," he told her, and got to his feet quickly. Looking down at her, he said, "Have another drink of water. I'm going to check things out."

She watched him walk away and marveled at how quietly such a big man could move. In seconds he was back. "Sun's gone down. Time to head out."

Lisa smothered a groan as he packed up the few things he'd carried with him. He gave her another drink of water, took one himself, then helped her to her feet.

"Better put my shirt back on," he said, snatching it up off the ground to hand to her. "Gonna be cold again in no time."

She slipped it on, then paused for a long look at the man standing within an arm's reach of her. His chest looked impossibly broad. His square jaw screamed defiance. The weapon he held was deadly. But the look in his eyes as he stared at her told Lisa that nothing and no one would hurt her.

And her bruised heart felt warm and full.

"Come on, princess, you're doin' fine."

She huffed out a breath that ruffled the bangs drooping over her forehead, but the glare she shot him let Travis know exactly what she was thinking. And he figured if she was carrying a gun, he'd have been a dead man a couple hours ago.

"How…far…have…we…come?" she asked, every breath interrupted with a gasp or a moan.

He took the hint and stopped. "A couple of miles."

"It feels like more," she said, and dropped to the ground. Staring up at him, she continued, "I hate to sound like a three-year-old in the back of a station wagon, but—how much longer?''

A brief smile crossed his face as he reached into his breast pocket for the map he'd already consulted several times. Going down on one knee beside her, he unfolded the thing, angled it to catch the moonlight and did some fast figuring. ''The city's still a ways, but we're almost in El Baharian territory.''

''That's good, right?''

''Right. Once we're safely on their side of the border, we can relax.''

''Relax. God, what a wonderful word.'' She sighed, pushed her hair back from her face, then rubbed at her calf.

Travis frowned and found himself wishing there were some other way. If he could contact his team, they'd be able to call in another chopper. But the throat mikes they wore on the mission were too short range to be of any use. Nope. They were on their own and that meant walking out. Whether it beat the princess into the ground or not.

''You're doin' great,'' he said, knowing she probably wouldn't care what he thought, but he had to at least give her this. He had to tell her that she'd done a better job of keeping up than a lot of boot Marines might have.

She slowly lifted her head and looked at him. ''Was that a compliment?''

He cleared his throat, scraped one hand across his face and when he'd stalled as long as possible, he muttered, "Yeah. I guess it was."

She stared up into his eyes and in the moonlight she looked too damn good. That pale-yellow dress of hers looked like spun gold in the silvery light. Her blond hair was messy and tumbled around her face in the kind of waves that made a man want to comb his fingers through them.

His mouth dried up, and it had nothing to do with the lack of water. Travis's insides were twisted into knots, and a hard ball of need settled down low in his gut. He wanted to pretend nothing was happening, but he was a man unused to lying. Even to himself.

And the truth of the matter was the princess was getting to him. Oh, she complained and argued, but hell, that only made the trip interesting. Beneath that spoiled-rich-girl exterior, there was a thread of steel. And that thread kept her moving despite her fear, her exhaustion. Hell, despite *him.*

"Thank you, Travis," she said and her voice came soft and quiet. "Strangely enough, coming from you, that actually means a lot to me."

He could see she meant that, and it pleased him. "You earned it."

"I know," she said, and gave him a smile that slammed into him with the force of mortar fire. But he shook the feeling off to listen to her. "I'm dirty and tired and sore, but I'm doing it. And I'm going to make it the rest of the way, too."

"Yeah," he agreed, nodding. "You will."

He handed her the canteen and offered her a drink. She took it gratefully, and after she'd handed it back, he took a swallow himself, letting the water soak into his dry mouth before allowing it to slide down his throat. It took care of his thirst, now all he could hope was it would cool the fire building inside him.

But the way he was feeling, he suspected that would take a lot more water. Say, a lakeful.

"Those shoes working better for you now?" He shifted the conversation, hoping to get his mind off his hormones as he carefully stowed the canteen.

"Yes." She drew one foot up and examined what was left of her expensive but useless footwear. "Although Ferragamo would have been highly insulted to see you using that knife of yours to whack at his creation."

Not as insulted as she had been, he was willing to wager. He could still see the look on her face when he'd sat her down and broken off the spindly heels. Personally, he was a fan of high heels. They did amazing things for women's legs—especially, he admitted silently, hers. But they weren't exactly made for trooping through the desert.

Along the horizon a sliver of pale blue edged the night. Sunrise was coming. Already the stars looked a bit less bright. Squinting, he narrowed his gaze and took in the surrounding area. For miles in every direction, there was simply nothing. They'd long ago left the rocky terrain behind and had entered the real desert. Sand dunes stretched out forever, and Travis knew they'd need to find some kind of shelter before morning. To be trapped on the sand during the day would be asking for trouble.

Not only would they be out in the open, they'd also be at the mercy of the sun. No caves around here, he thought, but there was something she'd probably like a hell of a lot better. Plus, it was in El Baharian territory. They'd be safe. And with any luck, they could make it there in just under a couple of hours.

Standing up again, he held out a hand toward her. "Time to go."

Obviously tired, she didn't even argue. She slapped her hand into his and moaned quietly when he pulled her to her feet. For one long moment she stood there, her hand in his. His thumb scraped across the tops of her knuckles, and he watched her shiver. Damn. He didn't know if it was good or bad that she was just as affected by a simple touch as he was.

Finally, though, she pulled her hand free, and Travis didn't even want to admit to himself just how empty his felt without hers in it.

Then she swayed unsteadily and fell into him. His arms came around her in an instinctive move and he heard her breath catch as her breasts pressed against his chest. Heat—pure, undiluted, hot-as-the-halls-of-hell heat—swamped him and he was pretty sure she felt it, too.

Their gazes locked for one long minute before she slowly…reluctantly, stepped back and away.

Damn.

"Okay," she said, her voice over-bright in a futile attempt to cover up the awkwardness of the moment. "Let's get this over with."

Travis nodded. Good idea, he thought, but knew he wouldn't forget the feel of her in his arms. "Right. If we set out at a good clip, we'll be able to make our next stop in about two hours."

"'Good clip,' eh?" she repeated with a smile. "Is that Marine-speak?"

"Close enough."

She put her hands at the small of her back and stretched, leaning her head back, staring up at the sky.

Travis, though, couldn't take his gaze off her. Even with his too-big shirt hanging off her slim body, she looked feminine enough to stoke the hunger riding him. Strange, he'd started out on this mission resenting her and now...hell, he didn't know what he thought anymore.

"Beautiful, isn't it?"

"What?"

She turned her head to look at him and waved one hand at the star-studded sky above them. "This. I mean, granted we're not here under the best of circumstances. And I'd probably enjoy this a lot more if I were standing on a balcony of a great hotel, but it really is beautiful here."

Travis tilted his head back to look at the wide expanse of glittering sky, taking a moment to enjoy the view, something he'd never done before while on a mission.

"The air's so clear here," she was saying, her voice a soft hush of sound in the night, "the stars look close enough for you to be able to reach out and grab a handful of them."

Amazing, he thought, watching her as she turned in a slow circle, taking in the spectacular night sky. Even in these conditions, she took the time to admire the night sky. He wouldn't have thought her the type to notice anything outside a department store. But then, she was surprising him a lot, wasn't she?

"Don't you think it's beautiful?" she asked again.

Travis looked at the woman beside him for a long moment before saying, "Yeah. Beautiful."

And he knew for damn sure he wasn't talking about the sky.

Six

***

"Water," Lisa said breathlessly, hardly daring to believe her own eyes. "It's water. Lots of it."

"Looks good, doesn't it?" Travis asked.

She glanced at him briefly, taking the time to notice the half smile curving his mouth as he watched her. A slow curl of something warm and liquid unwound inside her, and Lisa had to force herself to turn her gaze back on what had to be the most beautiful pool of water she'd ever seen. Standing at the crest of yet another hill made of sand, she stared down at the shallow valley below. And in the heart of that valley lay an honest to goodness oasis.

For some reason, she'd never considered them real. She'd thought of them as products of Hollywood, created when filmmakers needed a lush spot for the ever popular love scene. Yet there it was, sparkling in the vast expanse of brown, like an emerald tossed into the dirt.

Pale light kissed the horizon, signaling the rising of the sun, warning of the heat to come. But below, in that blessed valley, tall, slender palms grew in a semicircle around the pool of blue water. The silky fronds rustled merrily in the breeze and sounded to Lisa like applause—as if even the trees were welcoming her. Grass, actual grass, lined the banks leading down to the water's edge, and dozens of bushes and plants thrived here, in the middle of nothingness.

After days of living in a beige world filled with fear and exhaustion, just the sight of the oasis was enough to make her heart swell with relief.

"It's wonderful," she said, and heard her voice crack.

"Even better," Travis told her, "we're officially in El Bahar now."

She turned her head to look at him again. "You mean…"

He grinned. "We're safe."

Safe. They'd actually made it. Escaped her captors. Survived the desert. Tears stung Lisa's eyes, but she blinked them back. Ridiculous to cry now that it was all over. The time for tears would have been in the cave. Or when she was struggling to keep up with him as they crossed the sand. But to get all misty now, when their troubles were behind them made absolutely no sense.

The last few days crowded together in her mind. Images of Travis, guiding her through the darkness, arguing with her, feeding her, protecting her, rose up in her mind, one after the other. She owed him so much more than she could ever repay. How does a person go about thanking someone for their life?

Especially, how did *she* go about it, since she hadn't exactly made his job any easier.

"I can't believe it."

"You can check the map if you don't believe me." His voice teasing, he looked at her as if he knew exactly what she was thinking.

"It's not that," she told him with a smile, letting her gaze slide from his to the desert landscape behind them. It felt as though she'd been born in this desert. And though she'd never admit this out loud to anyone, there had been times when she'd doubted that she would ever leave it. Yet here they were. What was that old saying? "Bloodied, but not beaten?" Lisa smiled to herself and took her first easy breath since the morning she'd been kidnapped.

They'd come so far, she and Travis. In more ways than one.

She'd only known him a few short days, but in some ways, Lisa felt closer to this man than to anyone else she'd ever known. Amazing how a few days of intense living could make you feel so…attached to someone. Looking up into that rugged face with its strong lines and sharp planes, Lisa's heart turned over. He'd literally saved her life. He'd pushed her to find her own limits and then helped her surpass them.

"You did it," she finally said, staring into those chocolate eyes that were now so familiar to her.

His grin slowly faded as he shook his head. "No, princess, *we* did it."

She laughed shortly and heard the irony in the sound. "We, huh? Awfully generous, Captain America." She shifted her gaze back to the cool, green grass below them. Easier to admit this part if she wasn't looking at him. "You practically had to save me in *spite* of me."

He took her upper arm in a firm grip and turned her around to face him. Heat pushed through her bloodstream at his touch, quickening her breath, staggering her heartbeat. Her stomach did another slow flip-flop, and Lisa wondered if she would ever feel that sensation again once they'd gone their separate ways.

His thumb rubbed her skin before he released her, and Lisa didn't even want to think about the immediate loss of warmth.

"Don't be so hard on yourself," he said. "You stood up to it. Way better than some I've seen."

She'd like to believe that, Lisa realized. For once in her life she'd like to believe that she'd accomplished something on her own. Strange. Three weeks ago her biggest accomplishment to date had been arranging an impromptu dinner party for seventy-five of her father's closest friends. And she'd been pretty proud of herself for it, too.

Now, though, she'd been put to the test and she'd passed. She'd survived a kidnapping and a hostile desert. She'd eaten a snake, slept in a cave and managed to keep up with a professional warrior on a forced march. And though heaven knew it hadn't been easy, she'd made it.

A sense of pride filled her, and Lisa marveled at it. It had been so long since she'd been proud of herself for anything.

"We'll rest here today," he was saying, and Lisa pushed her thoughts aside to listen. "Head for the city when the sun goes down. If we're lucky, we won't have to walk the whole way in. Might run into one of the El Baharian desert patrols." He slung his weapon over his shoulder and held out a hand to her. As she took it, he folded his fingers around hers and said, "But for now, how about we go on down there and scoop up some of that water?"

An hour later Travis leaned back against a date palm and laid his weapon on the grass beside him. For the first time since this whole thing had started, he felt relaxed. Now that they were in El Bahar, he knew that even if there were pursuers in the desert somewhere behind them, they would never risk crossing the border to cause trouble.

Mission accomplished, he thought, and wondered why he didn't feel more relieved about that. He should be quietly celebrating. Hell, they were about to go their separate ways—at last. Two days ago he'd been able to think of nothing else. But now, watching Lisa at the water's edge, only a foot or two away, things were different. In the soft hush of early-morning light, she knelt on the grass, using his water-filled Kevlar helmet as a wash basin. Drawing his knees up, he rested his hands on them and watched as she lifted first one arm, then the other, smoothing fresh water along her skin.

His body tightened and his hands clenched into fists. Yep, it was a good thing the mission was nearly over, he told himself. He was starting to get *way* too fond of this woman. If someone had told him he'd be feeling like this a few days ago, he would have thought they were nuts.

But damned if she hadn't gotten under his skin. Her fierce stubbornness. Her dogged determination to not be beaten. Her willingness to argue at the drop of a hat—and the fact that he didn't intimidate her in the slightest. He admired her—and he hadn't expected to.

Not one of the spoiled rich girls he'd grown up around could have stood up to the past few days. They'd have wilted under the pressure. But Lisa'd only gotten stronger. Like steel tempered under fire, she'd faced the worst and come out better for it.

His gaze narrowed on her as she cupped her hands and splashed water on her face and neck. Lifting her chin, she stared up into the already brassy sky and let water droplets slide down her throat and beneath the neckline of her dress. She sighed and he felt it.

Damn it, he felt that sigh right down to his bones.

It was the first time he'd really seen her in daylight—and he had to admit, at least silently, that she was made for sunshine. Her blond hair, even as wet as it was now, looked like gold, and her fair skin was—

Travis frowned as a quick jolt of anger pulsed through him. In a few long strides he was kneeling down beside her.

She glanced at him, smiled and said, "It feels so good to wash all of this sand off that I…" Her voice trailed off as she looked into his eyes. "What is it? What's wrong?"

"You tell me," he ground out and half turned her until he could see at close range what he'd only just spotted. On her shoulder, a large purple bruise discolored her skin, and she flinched as his fingertips smoothed over it gently.

"Oh, that."

He hadn't seen it before. But then, since the moment they met, they'd been in the dark. Either at night, or in the cave. "Yeah, that."

"It's nothing. Just a bruise."

"They hit you?" he asked unnecessarily, fighting the urge to run back the way they'd come, find the SOBs and give them a few bruises.

She shrugged out from under his touch and looked over her shoulder at him. "Just one of them. Generally they treated me pretty well, considering. This was just the one time."

"Once is enough."

"Exactly my thoughts," she told him, and gave him a brave smile that tore at his heart. And she hadn't said a word of complaint about this, hadn't whined or asked for sympathy, despite the fact that her shoulder must have been hurting. There was a slender thread of iron in this woman, making her so much more than she seemed. Travis pictured her, alone, scared and facing down her captors. He was willing to bet she'd given as good as she got. Hell, she'd bitten him, and he was rescuing her. Maybe this was the only physical bruise she carried, but how many others stained her heart? Her soul? And she hadn't let them stop her, either. A swell of pride filled him.

He reached out again, giving in to his instincts, and this time caressed her cheek with his fingertips. Her eyes closed as he touched her, and he felt her tremble shake through him, too. Trouble, his brain shouted, but thankfully, his body wasn't listening. His blood felt as if it was boiling in his veins. Every breath staggered in and out of his lungs, and his heart pounded hard enough to shove through his rib cage. He wanted her. Needed her. Here. Now.

The slide of his fingers across her skin sent shafts of pure, white heat slicing through him and it was all he could do not to grab her, pull her close and cover her mouth with his. But despite the rush of need choking him, there was still a small, rational voice in the corner of his mind screaming at him to back off. This wasn't real. None of this. It was a world apart from reality. Like this oasis in the middle of a desert, his time with her was a spot of glory in the middle of an everyday life. And soon, they'd be back in civilization. Back to the real world— where he and the princess, under normal circumstances, would never have met.

He pulled back, but Lisa reached up and caught his hand in hers, holding it to her face, stroking her fingers along his. "Travis..."

"This'd be a big mistake," he said, his gaze shifting from her eyes to her mouth and back again.

She licked her lips, and his insides tightened even further. Which didn't really seem possible.

"It doesn't feel that way right now," she told him, and her voice was soft, welcoming.

"It will by tomorrow." He knew it. And if he had one active brain cell, he'd break this off and walk away now. While he still could.

She turned her face into his palm, then looked at him again. "All my life, I've worried about and planned for tomorrow. For once I'd just like to claim today and let tomorrow take care of itself."

An invitation.

One he couldn't have refused.

Even if he'd wanted to.

Pulling her closer, Travis bent his head. His gaze locked with hers, he moved in slowly, deliberately, giving her time to change her mind. Praying she wouldn't. Seconds ticked past. Closer. He inhaled her scent, warm and wet and woman. Closer still. Just a breath away now and he could almost taste her. She tipped her head back and leaned in toward him. Her blue eyes looked deeply into his, and Travis swore he could see straight into her soul.

Then their lips met, his eyes closed and thought stopped. Sensations poured through him, swamping him with the force of a tidal wave and he rode that swell, loving the ride. Gathering her tightly to him, his arms came around her as he deepened the kiss, parting her lips with his tongue, sweeping into her warmth, tasting her. She sighed into his mouth, and he took that small breath for his own, swallowing it and tucking it away inside him as though he might need that extra breath later.

Her tongue entwined with his, and she reached up, wrapping her arms around his neck, scraping her fingers across his nape. He shuddered at her touch, wanting more, needing more. Breaking the kiss, he dragged his lips along the line of her throat, tasting sand and fresh water and her soft, smooth skin. It fired his blood anew and sent desire pumping through him.

She moaned and tilted her head to one side, offering him access.

"Travis," she whispered, and her voice broke on his name. "Don't stop."

"Don't worry about that," he promised. Hungrily he moved his hands over her body, and she arched into his touch, silently urging him on. His fingers found the side zipper on her dress, and in an instant he'd pulled it down and slipped one hand beneath the torn yellow fabric. He cupped her breast and she gasped as the same, nearly electric shock of pleasure jolted them both. Her bra was nothing more than a bit of lace and a couple of straps. No match for a Marine.

His thumb caressed her hardened nipple through the lacy material, and she sighed his name, fueling the fires within. She filled him. His mind, his heart. All he could see and feel was her. This woman. This incredible woman who did things to him he never would have thought possible. Need roared up inside him, demanding to be fed.

He'd never known anything like it. Her passion simmered inside him, but it was more than that. He couldn't name it and didn't want to bother to try. It was enough that he could fill his hands and his heart with her.

Hands fumbling, mouths tasting, they pulled at each other's clothes in a frenzy to mate. To feel skin against skin, heat to heat. And when they were naked, he laid her back on the grass in a patch of shade thrown from the surrounding date palms.

A desert wind sighed across them, carrying the scent of the far-off sea and the heat of the sun. Travis speared his fingers through her hair, loving the feel of the silky, wet strands sliding over his skin. He cupped her face, turning her gaze to meet his. Reading the passion in her eyes, he dipped his head to hers and claimed another kiss. He took her, reveling in the feel of drowning in her warmth.

Lisa reached up and wrapped her arms around his neck, pulling him closer. She wanted to feel all of him pressed to her. His broad chest, sprinkled with a dusting of dark hair, was tanned and muscular. Soft and rough, hard and smooth, their bodies moved together, scraping flesh to flesh. Her fingers trailed down his back, loving the feel of him beneath her hands.

His callused palms moved down her length, stroking, caressing until Lisa writhed beneath him, lifting her hips, arching into him. Her legs parted in eager anticipation and when he touched her center, she groaned aloud.

Too much, she thought, her mind racing. It was all too much. Sensations escalated. Fire. Heat. A dazzling of sparks shooting through her blood. She looked into his eyes and saw a passion she'd never seen before. Five times she'd been engaged and yet she'd allowed none of her fiancés to touch her like this. There'd been no sparks. No magic. No hunger for more than the occasional kiss and cuddle.

She'd thought there was something wrong with her. Assumed that she was frigid. Accepted the fact that she lacked that certain something that made a woman want to be touched, explored, desired.

But there hadn't been anything wrong. She simply hadn't been with the right man.

Here, in this unlikely place, with a man who'd risked his life to save hers, she'd finally found him. And herself.

He dipped one finger into her heat and Lisa cried out, "Oh, Travis."

"I want you, darlin'," he said, his voice a whispered hush. "But—"

"But?" she repeated, suddenly terrified that he would stop touching her. That he would pull away before she knew the rest. Before she could finally experience what she'd waited all her life to feel. Had she finally found the right man only to have him turn from her?

"I don't have any protection," he said on a disappointed groan that shook her to her bones.

Her eyes flew open, and she stared into the chocolate depths looking down at her. "Protection?" Her brain had become so fuzzy she'd forgotten something that no woman should ever forget.

"Condoms." One corner of his mouth lifted into a sad smile. "Not exactly standard equipment for a recon mission."

Her body was tingling. His finger stroked that most sensitive piece of flesh and she quivered in his arms. Desperation rose up inside her. He couldn't stop. *They* couldn't stop. She had to finish this. Had to ease the ache building inside.

"It's okay," she murmured, lifting her hips into his hand, driving his finger deeper. "It's safe. I'm healthy."

"Me, too," he assured her, slipping another finger into her depths and stroking her body from the inside.

"Oh…" she sighed, licked her lips and asked, "Then what're we waiting for?"

"Am I glad to hear you say that," he said, and moved to cover her body with his.

Kneeling between her thighs, he shifted his hands to her bottom and lifted her hips high enough to ease his entry.

Lisa felt cherished, adored, and for that feeling she would risk anything. She tipped her head back into the grass, stared up at the lightening sky, then closed her eyes, the better to concentrate on what was about to happen to her.

He entered her body with one, swift, sure stroke and she gasped at the intimate invasion. So hard. So powerful. Like nothing she'd ever known before. And *so* worth waiting for. Her body ached and she felt herself stretching to accommodate him. After a few seconds ticked past, though, she began to wonder why he wasn't moving.

She opened her eyes to find him staring at her, irritation glittering in his dark-brown gaze.

"What is it?" she asked breathlessly. "What's wrong?"

"You're a virgin," he said flatly.

She smiled to herself, rocked her hips and took him deeper inside before saying, with some satisfaction, "Not anymore."

"You should have told me."

Ridiculous to be having this discussion now, she thought and moved again, twisting her hips this time until she saw a muscle in his jaw twitch as he tried for control.

"Could we—" she reached out to let her fingertips trail along his chest until that wall of muscle trembled "—talk about this...*later?*"

He groaned, clenched his teeth and nodded. "Right. Later. For sure."

"Oh, for sure."

He moved, rocking his hips, pushing himself so deeply inside her that she was sure she felt him touch her soul. He leaned over her, brushing his mouth over hers, then shifting to take first one nipple then the other into his mouth.

Lisa groaned, giving in to the spiraling whirl of feelings coursing through her. She felt as though she were racing through the darkness, headed for a glimmer of light that hung just out of her reach. Every aching muscle in her body strained for it. Tension built in a rush. He pushed her higher and higher, and when Lisa thought she couldn't stand the suspense any longer...the fireworks began.

The tingling deep inside built into a shower of sparks that cascaded through her, splintering the imagined darkness, covering her in bright, glorious color. So much more than she'd ever expected. So much better than she'd hoped. And it was all because of him. This one man who'd crept into her heart and carved his name there.

He felt her body climax, and the contractions shimmered through him, urging him to completion. And it was completion, he thought, staring down into those lake-blue eyes of hers. It was a homecoming. To a place he'd never been before.

To a place he never wanted to leave.

Her gaze locked with his as he emptied himself into her, and when he murmured her name, she cradled him in her arms and softened his fall.

Seven

He wasn't sure how long they lay there, but it was long enough for the sun to shift and the skimpy shade to swing wide of them. The sun poured down from a clear, empty sky and bathed them both in a heat that burned.

Rousing himself, Travis held on to her tightly and rolled them off into the shade again. The cool of the grass pressed against his back as he stared up at her, lying flat on top of him. "So," he said, "it's later. Talk."

She stretched and damn near purred, rubbing her legs and upper body against him until he felt himself go hard and ready again.

Okay, this wasn't going to work. If he expected to talk to her, then he'd better keep some distance between them. A couple thousand miles ought to do it.

He set her to one side, rolled away and snatched up his clothes. Then, tossing her dress and underthings to her, he said flatly, "Talk."

She sighed and he got the message. She plainly didn't want to have this conversation. But she should have told him. Maybe it would have stopped him from making love to her. Maybe not, but she should have said something.

Throwing her a quick glare over his shoulder, he yanked on his clothes. "Why didn't you tell me?"

"It's not exactly something I advertise, you know."

Damn, she didn't even look embarrassed to be lying naked in the dappled shade. For a recent ex-virgin, she was getting the hang of this sensuality thing real quick. Which brought him right back to the question at hand.

"How could you be a virgin?" he demanded, throwing his hands wide as he turned for another eye-popping look at her. "Do you live in a city filled with blind men?"

One corner of her mouth lifted. "Thanks. I think."

"Oh, it was a compliment, believe me." He

pulled his socks on, then reached for his combat boots. "But I don't get it. Have you been locked up in a convent or something?"

He heard her clothing rustle as she dressed and tried to keep from imagining her breasts as she hooked her bra.

"Of course not."

"Then what the hell were you waiting for?"

"It's not that I was *waiting*, exactly. The point is," she was saying, "I just never...*wanted* sex. I've never met anyone who—I mean I never wanted them to—I sort of figured I was frigid."

"Hah!" He couldn't help it. The short, sharp laugh shot from his throat before he could choke it off. He tied up one boot, then looked at her. Her pale skin looked tempting beneath that scrap of lace—and just a little pink. He'd rolled her out of the sun just in time. His hands itched to hold her again. His mouth watered at the thought of tasting her, and other parts of his body stood up at full attention. *"Frigid?* Honey, if you were any hotter, you'd have melted me."

A smug smile curved her mouth as she tugged her dress over her head. The worn fabric hid her body from him, and Travis figured that was just as well. Keep them both out of any more trouble. They had plenty enough already.

"So, it was...good."

It wasn't a question and yet it was.

"Beyond good," Travis said, and knew it for the understatement of the century. "But you know that."

"Yes, I do. What I don't know is why you're making such a huge deal out of this," she said. "We're both grown-ups. We made a choice—which I for one, don't regret for a single minute."

"This isn't about regrets."

"You could have fooled me."

"I didn't say I regretted anything."

"Then for heaven's sake, Travis, what exactly are you saying?"

He pushed one hand across the top of his head, stared off into the distance for a long moment before turning to glance at her briefly. "The plain truth is," he continued, tugging on his other boot and tying it up, "this changes things."

"Like what?" she asked. He turned around again to look at her.

"First off," he started, and it pained him to even say the words, "I'm thinking that if you were a virgin, you weren't 'safe.'"

"As a virgin," she pointed out, "I was perfectly safe. I've hardly been able to contract any diseases, now have I?"

"No," he agreed, "but you may have just contracted a baby."

She blew a puff of air at him and waved her hand dismissively. "Please. Women try for years to get pregnant. One time is hardly going to do the trick."

"I'm willing to bet lots of 'happy couples' have told themselves that."

"You're worrying over nothing," she told him, and yanked the zipper of her dress up.

"And you're not worrying at all," he countered.

"What would be the point?"

"Excuse me?"

"Well, whether I worry or not, the damage is done, so why worry ahead of time?"

"And how comfortable is your head, stuck so firmly in the sand?"

One pale-blond eyebrow lifted. "I'm not going to let you spoil this for me."

"Spoil it?"

"That's right. I've waited all my adult life for this experience, and now that I've had it, you're not going to ruin the memory of it."

"Well pardon the hell outa me."

"It won't be easy," she told him, giving him a look that could have fried bacon, "but I'll try."

He snatched up his weapon, slung it over his shoulder, then pushed himself to his feet. Staring down at her, Travis's gaze flicked over her thoroughly, from the top of her still-damp head to the soles of her feet. And it was all he could do not to grab her up and start the magic all over again.

But he called on years of training and withstood the urge. Barely. This was *so* not good. He'd finally met the woman who not only electrified his body but touched his heart—and she was farther away now than ever. There was no future here. He knew it. And so, he suspected, did she.

Marines and debutantes just did not mix.

"Listen, princess—*Lisa,*" he corrected, "you're my mission, not my date. I screwed up here and—"

"Oh, thank you very much," she snapped, scrambling to her feet so that she could glare right into his eyes. And it was quite a glare.

"All right," he admitted, "that came out wrong."

She folded her arms over her chest and tapped her foot in the sand. "Was there a *right* way to say that?"

"Probably not," he muttered, wondering how this mission had gone so wrong so completely? From the minute he'd slipped into that shack to free her, it seemed as though everything had gone against them. Missing their ride. Having to hide out. Hiking across the desert. And now this. But this he had no excuse for. This he'd done all on his own.

And as much as he knew it had all been a mistake, he still couldn't find it in himself to regret it. But what now? Walk away as though nothing had happened? Hell, yes. That was really his only choice. He didn't fit into her world any more than she would fit into his.

Lisa clung to what was left of her pride and wrapped it tightly around her slightly bruised heart. Well, this was just what a girl wanted to hear the minute her lover put his clothes on. She'd waited years for this moment only to have the one man who turned her blood into fire tell her he was sorry it had happened. Perfect.

Tears burned at the backs of her eyes, but she refused to let them fall. Through sheer will and determination, she held them back. It was bad enough knowing that he thought of their time together as a mistake. She wouldn't make her humiliation any worse by turning into a teary female.

Instead, she fell back into comfortable, familiar territory and shut off the emotions clamoring to get out. Over the years, she'd had plenty of practice at hiding what she was feeling. Her father had never approved of "scenes."

"Why don't we just pretend none of this happened?" she offered, though her body still hummed from his touch.

"That won't solve anything."

"There's nothing to solve."

"And if there's a baby?" he demanded. "Will you ignore that, too?"

She flushed at the direct hit and supposed she'd deserved it. But wasn't this what he wanted? Wasn't he looking for a way to distance himself? Well, there it was…being handed to him on one of her father's silver platters. You'd think he'd take the opportunity and run with it.

"*If* there's a baby, and that's a big if…" There wouldn't be, she told herself firmly. The gods simply weren't that cruel. "…I'll take care of it."

Now it was his turn to flush. In anger. She watched color race up to fill his cheeks and spark like fire from his eyes. His hands fisted at his sides, and she had the distinct feeling that he wanted to punch something. Badly.

"Just like that," he said through gritted teeth. "You'll take care of it."

"Yes." Oh, she knew what he was thinking—and it showed how little he really knew her. He'd assumed that she would hustle herself off for an abortion. But Lisa would never be able to do that. Not that she didn't sympathize with women who were forced to make such a heartrending decision. She did. But for herself, she simply wasn't capable of ending a life just to make her own more comfortable.

No, if she was pregnant, then she would be a mother. The word slammed into her mind and made her knees quake just a bit. She'd always wanted children. Although she had to admit that her fantasy of a family had always included a husband. Still, as she'd so recently discovered, not everything turned out the way you wanted it to.

"You're a real piece of work, you know that?" he muttered darkly and took a step closer.

That stung, but she didn't let him know it. Lifting her chin, she met him glare for glare. "Then it's lucky for you that you're almost rid of me, isn't it?"

"Princess," he said, his gaze flicking over her, "you have no idea."

Her breath hitched, and a small twinge of pain shimmered inside. But she didn't have to worry about him seeing it reflected in her expression. He'd already turned his back on her. She watched him stalk across the grass and climb the sand hill that surrounded this little valley. At the crest he sat down, pulled his weapon across his lap and stared out into the distance.

Her lover was gone.

Her guard dog was back.

And inside, Lisa wept.

The desert patrol spotted them an hour later.

Travis was all business as he briefed the king's men on the situation, then climbed into the back of the Jeep, putting himself as far away from her as possible. Lisa smiled and said all the right things, but her mind was working independently of her speech. Every thought was of Travis and what would happen now. Would he disappear the moment they hit the American Embassy? Would he even remember her a month from now? Would he want to?

The Jeep hit a rut in the road, and her back teeth jarred together. Reaching out, she grabbed hold of the edge of the windshield and braced herself. Too late, of course. Just as she'd been too late to protect her heart from Travis Hawks.

The marble foyer of the embassy felt cool and the sleek elegance of the building brought home the fact that they were back in civilization. The El Baharian soldiers had called ahead, letting the embassy know they were coming in.

Travis stood back as the Ambassador himself scuttled forward to greet Lisa. The man barely spared Travis a glance as he said, "Miss Chambers, I'm delighted to see that you're well and safe."

"Thank you, Mr. Ambassador," she murmured, but her soft voice echoed in the vastness of the place.

How sophisticated she sounded, Travis thought, remembering how she'd screeched at him out in the desert. But then, that was a different Lisa from this one. And damned if he didn't already miss that other woman. The one he'd come to know. To...care for.

He shook his head and told himself he'd had too

much sun. It wasn't affection he felt for her. It was just the kind of camaraderie that developed between people when they shared a tense situation. They'd survived together. But they sure as hell didn't belong together.

"Sergeant..." the Ambassador tacked a question mark onto that single word.

"Hawks, sir," he answered. "Travis Hawks."

"Of course," the little man said. "The other members of your team are waiting for you. If you'll follow my secretary..." He waved one hand to indicate a tall man in his forties.

"Thank you, sir," Travis said and started after the secretary, already heading down a long hallway. He didn't look back at Lisa. He'd learned long ago that looking back only made things worse. Better to keep his gaze fixed straight ahead. On the future that wouldn't include Lisa Chambers.

"Gunnery Sergeant Hunter thought you'd be hungry first," the man in front of him said. "If you go through that door there, you'll find the kitchen."

Food. Drink. Sounded good. The only thing that would make it better was if Lisa was with him. But she'd probably have servants trotting a meal up to her in no time. "Thanks," he said with a nod, then pushed through the door.

"Well speak of the devil and in he walks," Deke shouted with a wild laugh.

"He sure looks like he's been to hell and back," J.T. agreed as he hurried over to slap Travis's back with a solid thump of welcome.

"Never thought I'd be glad to see your ugly faces again," Travis told them, shaking hands with the best friends he'd ever had.

"Hawks," Jeff Hunter said from across the room.

Travis snapped the other man a quick look. A Gunnery Sergeant, Jeff was the Senior NCO and the man in charge of their recon team.

The man's stern features dissolved into a grin. "We're damn glad to see you, Travis."

"Likewise, Gunny." He dropped his pack unceremoniously to the floor, tossed his weapon to Deke and headed for the other man. Shaking the hand he offered, Travis asked the question that had been haunting him for a few days now. "The Marine who got hit on the chopper? How is he?"

"Don't worry about him," Jeff said with a smile. "Took one in the shoulder and he may even get some liberty to recuperate. He wanted me to thank you for getting him a trip home."

"That's good news, Gunny," Travis said, feeling a rush of relief push through him.

"Could have been worse if you hadn't waved us off," Jeff told him, meeting his gaze and holding it for a long minute. "You made the right call."

"Thanks. Just glad it worked out." Sort of, he added silently.

"Man," J.T. was saying, "it must have been pure torture putting up with little miss rich—"

One hot look from Travis cut that phrase off before it could be finished. "She did all right," he said, shifting his gaze from one to the other of the Marines standing around him. "She stood up to it. She really came through."

"So did you," Jeff said, and gave him another slap on the back strong enough to stagger a slighter man. "And now that that's all taken care of, you hungry?"

"Gunny," Travis said with feeling, "I could eat one of those camels we passed on the way in. Hide, hump, hooves and all."

"Not necessary," Jeff told him. "We may be in El Bahar, but the embassy is American territory. Take a look at what the chef cooked up for you and Miss Chambers."

Travis looked over at a gleaming stainless-steel countertop that was piled high with enough food to make a fair-size banquet. His mouth watered as he muttered, "Fried chicken, potato salad, watermelon, strawberry shortcake and chocolate chip cookies." He glanced at Jeff. "Is Lisa—Miss Chambers being fed now, too?"

"As we speak."

"All right, then." He sighed heavily, pushed his friends out of the way and said, "I've died and gone to heaven, fellas. If this is a dream, don't wake me up."

Eight

Everyone was asleep.

The muted roar of the jet's engines pulsed just below the chorus of snores reverberating from the front few seats. Travis pushed himself from the plush leather chair and walked down the length of the richly appointed plane toward the galley.

His worn, dirty boots sank into the thick, sky-blue carpet, and his gaze flicked over his surroundings with interest. Lisa hadn't even had to request her father's private jet. Mr. Chambers, on hearing that his only child was safe, had dispatched his plane to carry her, and the recon team that had saved her, home. And Travis had never seen such accommodations.

Charcoal-gray leather captain's chairs were scattered around the front of the plane and three of them were fully reclined, allowing the Marines to snooze on their way home. An overstuffed couch hugged one wall of the plane. On the other wall a desk was outfitted with a fax machine, computer and printer. A mahogany bar took up most of the wall at the front of the jet, and he'd been told that the door in the rear led to a bedroom complete with queen-size bed and master bath.

He shook his head, hardly able to believe that people actually lived like this. And at that thought, a flash of himself, traveling in military transport planes rushed up in his mind, and he almost laughed aloud at the comparison. But the urge to laugh died as quickly as it came when he realized that the plane was a tangible example of just how little he and the princess had in common.

Travis's back teeth ground together, and he told himself it didn't matter. What they'd shared was over. As it should be. The fact that he wished it wasn't didn't mean a damn thing.

He quickened his step, headed for the galley, just past the desk. He didn't feel like sleeping. He'd done plenty of that at the embassy. And since Lisa was back in the bedroom, and his friends were snoring loudly enough to wake the dead, coffee seemed like just the right ticket.

As he came around the corner, Travis stopped short and felt every nerve ending in his body go on full alert.

Lisa stood there, looking as different from the woman he'd come to know as night was from day. Gone was the torn, dirty dress and the tangled mass of blond curls. She wore the clothes her father had sent to her. Some sort of filmy, light-blue dress with a skirt tight enough to drive a man crazy, thinking of ways to peel it off her. The pale-blue spike heels she wore brought her much closer to his own height than she had been the past few days and did absolutely amazing things for her legs. Her shining blond hair was pulled back from her face with a diamond clip that glittered like chips of ice in the overhead lights. There was no spark of irritation shining in those blue eyes anymore—now there was only a cool sophistication that he simply had no idea how to relate to.

But even as that last thought registered, the expression in her eyes shifted, changing, and just for an instant she was his princess. The woman he'd known so intimately in a setting that should have killed them both. In a heartbeat, though, that change was gone and she was a beautiful stranger again.

''I, uh,'' he said, trying to find a way to cover his

own reaction to her, "I didn't know you were back here. Just came for some coffee."

Nodding, she picked up a delicate china cup, set it on its matching saucer and filled it from the nearby glass carafe. Steam rose from the surface of the coffee cup as she handed it to him. But that heat was nothing compared to what sizzled between them as her hand brushed his.

She jerked back quickly, sloshing some of the inky black liquid over the cup's lip. "Sorry," she murmured, picking up a linen napkin and handing it to him.

"No problem," he said. After blotting up the mess he tossed the napkin aside. He allowed his gaze to sweep her up and down, and he felt the sharp jolt of need slam home in his gut. Well, he'd just have to get used to ignoring that, he told himself. There was no help for it now. They were on their way home. Back where she lived a life of luxury on Park Avenue and he...*didn't.*

And just to drive himself totally insane, an image of her naked, lying on the banks of the oasis, leaped into his mind. The memory was so clear he could almost feel the silky softness of her skin. A sudden tension crashed through him, and Travis immediately let that vision go. No peace there, he reminded himself.

It was stupid of him to feel so uncomfortable

around her. When two people had gone through
what they had, side by side, they should be able to
talk to each other civilly, for Pete's sake. Determined to prove to both himself and to her that it was
possible, he leaned one hip against the tiled counter,
took a sip of coffee and watched her as he com-
mented, "Quite a plane."

Oh, yeah, Hawks. That was brilliant.

"My father likes it," she said, picking up her own
coffee.

"So do the guys," he said wryly.

The other men's combined snores drifted toward
them, and Lisa smiled briefly. "It is comfortable for
long trips."

"It's got military transport beat down to the
ground, I'll give you that."

"Bad, huh?"

He shrugged. "War's hell, but it still beats transport."

A smile tugged at the corner of her lips and set
up an answering tug deep inside him. Damn, she got
to him like no other woman ever had. And he'd been
a fool to let it go as far as it had. Now he'd be
paying the price for letting down his guard.

Yep, when she got back home and resumed her
life, partying, going to lunch and forgetting all about
him, Travis had the distinct feeling that he was going to be haunted by dreams of her. By thoughts of

what might have been. He could wish it were different, but as his grandfather used to say, "If wishes were horses, beggars would ride."

"So," he said, his voice overly loud in an effort to quiet the voices in his mind, "how's it feel to get back to reality?"

Lisa lifted her chin, took a deep breath and looked up at him. He felt the solid punch of her gaze right down to the soles of his feet.

"The desert felt more real."

Lisa meant it. Looking into those chocolate eyes of his, she realized just how much she'd missed seeing them in the past twenty-four hours. Since entering the city of El Bahar, she and Travis had been kept separate, through accident or design. She wasn't sure which.

All she was sure of was that she'd missed him. Missed arguing with him. Missed the way he smiled. The way he seemed to stand so much taller than any other man she'd ever met. Missed knowing that he was there. By her side. Ready to protect and defend.

The men in her world wore three-piece suits, showed up at the "right" parties and bought and sold Fortune 500 companies before breakfast. Yet none of them carried themselves with the kind of self-confidence Travis did. None of them would even have risked lunch for her sake, let alone their lives.

And, she thought with an inward groan, none of them were capable of starting a flash fire in her bloodstream, cithcr.

He'd touched her in so many ways. In a few short days Travis Hawks had managed to march into her life, her heart and her soul. And she was pretty sure there'd be no getting him out again.

Which was going to make for a very lonely life.

"You did great out there," he was saying, and she pushed away her thoughts to concentrate on what little time she had left with him. "In the desert, I mean," he finished.

Pride swelled inside her briefly, but she pushed it back down again. It was only through his and God's efforts that she'd ever made it out of the desert alive. Even now the memory of fear was fading, along with the sense of accomplishment she'd experienced in keeping up with her rescuer.

Here, in the safety of her father's jet, surrounded by the luxury she'd grown up in, all of it seemed so far away. So unreachable. Even Travis. He was right here in front of her. And yet she knew that the moment he'd seen this stupid plane, he'd distanced himself further from her. She'd watched the Marines' reactions to the jet. Seen the awe in their faces. And she'd seen cold, hard realization come into Travis's eyes and knew that she'd lost him. For good.

Better now to pretend she'd never had him. She laughed shortly and shook her head. "Thanks, but I think we both know that without you it would have been a different story."

"Yeah, but you weren't trained how to survive that kind of thing."

"True enough," she agreed, and plastered a wide, phony smile on her face. "But you should see me at a designer's show. I'm known as the fastest draw of a credit card on the eastern seaboard."

"Cut it out."

The snap in his voice had her blinking in surprise. "What?"

He set his coffee cup down with a clatter, then reached out and grabbed her upper arms. Lisa felt the hot, hard strength of him pouring down into her bones, and she wanted to sway against him. To bring back the memories of their time together. To relive it. To experience the magic again. But his features were just as tight as his grip, so she swallowed those feelings back.

"Don't start pretending again."

"Pretending?"

"Yeah," he said, and loomed over her, his face just a breath—or a kiss—away. "Don't start trying to play the dimwit rich girl. Not with me. Don't pretend to be less than you are."

"Who's pretending?" she asked, and pulled free

of his grasp. The sudden lack of warmth from his hands chilled her and made her just a little bit lonelier than she had been. But she knew she'd better get used to that. "You called it from almost the moment we met. You said I was a spoiled princess. You said all I had going for me was daddy's money."

He winced.

"No point in backing down now," she continued, saying aloud what she knew he'd been thinking. "We are who we are, Travis. You're Daniel Boone and I'm...I'm..." She shook her head. "I don't know who I am anymore."

"Well I do," he said tightly, bending down low so that they were eyeball to eyeball. His voice came in a rush of hushed anger that rolled over her, pushing his words deep inside her. "You're Lisa Chambers. And that's a helluva lot more than I gave you credit for being. You're tough and beautiful and strong and so damn sexy I want you again, right here."

Her knees wobbled and her stomach pitched.

"You've pissed me off and you've made me proud," he said, and darned if she didn't feel tears burning the backs of her eyes. She couldn't ever remember hearing someone tell her they were proud of her before. And the words acted like a salve on a wound she hadn't known she carried. She blinked those tears back quickly but apparently not before he'd seen them.

Straightening up, Travis took a half step back from her, and she wanted to tell him not to go. To stay close. Because when he was around, she felt like the kind of person she used to dream of being.

"Look," he said, reaching up to shove one hand across the top of his head. "We've been through a lot together, that's all. So don't put yourself down, cause I know better."

She swallowed hard and wished she could throw her arms around him.

"And there's something else," he said, making Lisa's breath catch in her throat.

What? Was he actually going to say something about a future? Would he tell her that he cared? Did she *want* him to care? Oh yes. Yes, she did. Because as strange a thing as it was to admit, she'd fallen in love with the hard-core Marine with the slow, Southern slide in his voice.

She wouldn't have thought it possible to love so suddenly. So completely. So surely. But it was there. Within her. Nestled like a nugget of pure-gold knowledge. Travis Hawks was the one man in the world for her. Hopefully, he felt the same.

"What's that, Travis?" she asked.

He glanced back down the wide aisle as if to assure himself that his friends were still asleep. When he was satisfied, he turned his gaze back to her and said quietly, "Until I know for sure that you're not pregnant, I'm going to be a part of your life whether you like it or not."

Every bit of air left her body. Not in a rush. It slipped out, like air leaking from a balloon. And just like that, her tidy little vision of a cozy cottage built for two dissolved.

Disappointment gave way to anger and anger to rage. In seconds it was pumping through her bloodstream, looking for a way out. How could she have been so stupid? Why was *he* so stupid? Didn't he see that they belonged together? Didn't he feel the same magic when they touched?

"*That's* what you had to tell me?"

"Yeah," he said, surprise etched on his features as he recognized the fury in her tone. "What'd you think?"

She hadn't been thinking at all, she told herself. She'd been dreaming. Wrapped up in a ridiculous little dream in which he loved her. Hurt and anger simmered inside until it came to a boil, making every breath a superhuman effort. She trembled with the force of it and still had to fight back tears of disappointment and frustration.

Which only made her angrier.

"What I *think*, Travis Hawks," she said, every

word dropping like an icy stone, "is that *you* are an idiot!"

"Huh?"

She pulled her right foot back, then slammed the toe of her brand-new shoe into his left shin.

"Ow! Hey!"

He grabbed for his injured leg, and Lisa limped past him as if he were a stone statue. Her toes throbbed, but the pain was worth it. She only wished she'd been able to kick as high as his thick head.

Nine

They were met in D.C. by Lisa's father, a three-star General and of course the media. There were far fewer reporters than Lisa had expected yet more than Travis was comfortable with.

As the plane's door swung open, cameras flashed frantically in the night. A strobe light effect accompanied Lisa as she walked down the stairway to the tarmac. Her gaze shifted automatically to her father. Alan Chambers impatiently checked the time on his Rolex, then muttered something to the General beside him before starting forward to meet his daughter.

Right behind her, Lisa heard Travis and his friends taking the metal stairs with hurried steps. Apparently they were more eager to get back to the real world than she felt at the moment.

"Lisa." Her father's booming voice came, loud enough to be picked up by the television cameras cordoned off more than thirty feet away.

She flicked a quick glance at the reporters, then looked back at her father. Tall, black hair streaked with gray, Alan Chambers was an imposing figure. At least, he'd always intimidated her. Not that he didn't love her, she thought, defending him. He did. In his way. But he was a busy man, with his sights set on a seat in the Senate.

"Hi, Dad," she said as he came close enough to wrap her in a brief, tight hug. She inhaled his familiar scent: fine cigars, breath mints and woodsy aftershave. And just for a minute she wished that hug would go on. That her father would hold her and tell her everything would be all right. That she wouldn't miss Travis even before he was gone.

But he patted her back awkwardly, then stepped away, holding her at arm's length, where, she thought with an inward sigh, he'd always kept her. Still, his smile was warm and his eyes shone as he said, "Honey, how are you?"

"I'm fine. Really." A little bruised around her heart, but at least it didn't show.

"I can't tell you how worried I was," he was saying, his gaze lifting to look at the Marines assembling behind her. "No more shopping trips for a while, okay?"

She gave him the smile he expected, even though he wasn't looking at it. "Good idea." Then, steeling herself, she half turned and said, "Dad, I'd like you to meet Travis Hawks. He's the man who brought me out of the desert."

Travis stepped forward and shook the man's hand, barely glancing at Lisa. "Sir."

"Sergeant, good to meet you." Her father's gaze drifted past Travis to the others. "Good to meet all of you. I want to thank you for rescuing my wayward daughter."

Travis frowned slightly but was careful not to show it. He'd expected Lisa's father to be just a bit more glad to see her. But then, Mr. Chambers might be the private type, preferring to do his celebrating out of the glare of the media. Travis couldn't blame him any for that. The continuous flicker of camera lights was annoying.

"Marines," the General spoke up next. "Well done."

"Thank you, sir," Jeff replied, snapping to and returning a salute.

"Indeed," Mr. Chambers said. "The General,

here, informs me that you've all been given two weeks of leave.''

The men grinned.

''And to make sure you understand how grateful I am, I'd like you all to be my guests at the Sheraton. Take some time to relax, enjoy yourselves.''

Lisa's gaze shot to Travis, and he felt the power of it slam home to his gut. Two more weeks with her. Was that a good or a bad thing? Probably a little of both.

''Thank you, sir,'' Jeff said, glancing at Deke and J.T., ''but if it's all the same to you, I think the team would rather take the two weeks with their families.''

Mr. Chambers looked shocked for a second or two, as if he was a man not used to hearing the words *no, thanks*. But to give him his due, he recovered quickly enough, nodding sharply at Jeff before fixing a steady stare on Travis. ''I'm disappointed,'' he said, ''but of course I understand. However, I would appreciate Sergeant Hawks staying in town a few days at least. As the man most directly responsible for my daughter's rescue, I'd like to thank him personally.''

Travis opened his mouth to turn him down. First off, he didn't answer to Alan Chambers. Second, he didn't want or need thanks for doing his job. Besides, staying in D.C. meant staying near Lisa, and that probably wasn't a good idea. Leaving now would be for the best, he knew.

No point in hanging on to something that was already dead and buried, right? But then his gaze caught Lisa's. In those lake-blue eyes he read regret and goodbye. A jolt of something sad and sweet pinged around his insides. Before he could stop himself, he said, "Be happy to, sir."

"Excellent," her father crowed.

Her eyes softened just a little, but before Travis could figure out exactly what that meant, her father had grabbed him and turned him toward the flashing cameras. Dropping one arm around Travis's shoulder, Mr. Chambers drew Lisa in close on his other side. Then he gave them each a squeeze and ordered, "Smile now, you two."

Travis felt like a bug under a magnifying glass. And the ache in his heart could have been the pin, jammed through his body, keeping him in place.

How easy it was to slip back into old patterns.

After more than two weeks in a desert, where Lisa's strength of will had been her greatest weapon in the quest to stay alive, she was right back where she started. Here, in this mint-green room, her will wasn't needed or wanted. Here she was what her father expected her to be.

"Thank you, Patti," she said as the maid set a

breakfast tray down on a nearby table. Amazing. A few days ago she had been crouched in a cave eating a snake. Today there was steaming coffee and toast on a silver tray.

"Oh, you're welcome, ma'am," the woman said on her way out the door again. "We're all so glad you're back home safely."

Lisa forced her lips up a notch or two into what she hoped would pass as a smile. It was simply the best she could do at the moment. Fatigue dragged at her. Through snatches of sleep, Travis's image had haunted her. His eyes, his smile, his touch. And finally, staying in that wide, empty bed had just been too much for her.

From her vantage point on the plush window seat, she'd watched the sun rise, brushing pale color across the sky as it wiped away the last of the stars. In the desert, the sunrise had been followed by quiet, the promise of blistering heat and a day spent in hiding. Here, the city was coming to life, cars and people rushing down the avenue, everyone in a hurry to get somewhere they would hurry home from in a few hours.

And tomorrow would be the same. Within a few days her life would return to normal. She'd pick up the threads of her everyday routine and go on as if nothing had ever happened to disrupt it. Travis would be gone, back to duty. And she would be…here.

She should be happy. Or at least relieved. She was safe. Home. Frowning to herself, she stood up, crossed to the tray and poured herself a cup of coffee. Holding the cup between her palms, she walked back to the French doors leading onto the small balcony. Stepping outside, she shivered as an early-morning breeze sailed past, tugging at the hem of her sapphire-blue silk robe. She took a sip of the hot coffee, walked to the rail and stopped.

Restlessness clawed at her. The familiar felt strange now, and she found herself thinking fondly of that desert trek. Here she was what she'd always been. Alan Chambers's daughter. An attractive woman who knew how to throw a good party.

With Travis she'd discovered another Lisa. A Lisa she'd thought had faded away years ago. There in the desert, when they were struggling to survive… counting on each other…helping each other…she'd felt *alive* for the first time in way too long.

And in Travis's arms she'd discovered what it was like to really love.

But now it was over, and the man who'd touched her as no one else ever had was probably counting the minutes until he could get away.

Setting her coffee cup down on the wide railing,

Lisa gripped the scrolled metal in both hands. The cold of the black iron seeped into her bones until she felt as chilled outside as she did within. Pulling in a long, deep breath, she threw her head back and stared at the lightening sky as she tried to adjust to the heaviness in her heart.

"You'd better get used to it," she muttered. "Once Travis is out of your life, that feeling's going to be with you a long time."

Hearing the words aloud made her question them, though. Frowning, she thought, why *should* she let him go? Who said she *had* to go back to being the woman she'd been before all this started? Slowly, thoughtfully, she straightened up, shifting her gaze back to the stream of cars out on the avenue. Blindly she watched as motorists flicked off their headlights in deference to the brightening sun. But she wasn't seeing the traffic at all. Instead, she looked inward and found the memory of a pair of chocolate eyes that watched her with desire and admiration.

Her heart twisted, and a slow, sweet ache unwound through her. She missed him. She missed who she was when she was with him. And darn it, she didn't want her old life back. She wanted a new life. A new start. With Travis.

"I'm not going to lose him," she said, her tone strengthening with each word. "I won't." Her grip on the railing tightened until she wouldn't have been surprised to find the cold black metal snapping in her hands. Resolve filled her. Excitement fluttered in the pit of her stomach. And anticipation dried her mouth and made her heart beat wildly.

She could do this.

She could convince Travis that they belonged together.

Sure he was stubborn. But she could be just as hardheaded when it came to something she really wanted. All she'd need was time. But all she had were a few short days.

"This was a mistake."

Travis slapped one hand against the wall and leaned into the wind rushing past him through the opened window. Air-conditioning might be popular with most people, but he was a man who needed fresh air. It kept his head clear and helped him focus. And God knew, he needed all the help he could get at the moment.

He had to figure out how to dig himself out of the hole he'd leaped into.

The quiet of his hotel room strained on his nerves. But he was in no mood for the artificial company of the television set. If Jeff and the guys had stayed in town, it might have been easier to stay distracted. But as it was, all he could think about was Lisa. And that wasn't going to do him any good.

He glared down at the stream of traffic on the streets below and envied the people in those cars. At least they were on familiar turf. Going about their business. Getting things done. Not him.

"Nope," he muttered. "Travis Hawks *should* be hightailing it back to Texas, but instead he's hanging around to spend time with a woman he might have made pregnant."

But even as he said it, he knew that wasn't the only reason he was still here, where he so clearly didn't belong. He wasn't thinking about some phantom child. It was Lisa's face that stayed in the front of his mind. Her laughter. Her touch. Her sharp tongue and hard head.

His gut tightened and his breath clogged in his lungs. This was his own damned fault. He'd let her in. Allowed her to become important. To matter. Pregnant or not, Lisa Chambers had made her way into his heart and he didn't have the first clue about how to get her out.

The worst of it was, he wasn't at all sure he *wanted* her out. Oh, he knew there was no future for them. They were miles apart in every way imaginable. And if he hadn't known it before, he would have had to acknowledge it the moment he'd seen the media greeting their return from El Bahar. Her father was news. And by association so was she.

She hadn't grown up with a silver spoon in her

mouth. Hell, she'd had the whole damn set of flat-ware. They were from different worlds. She'd never be satisfied with his, and he had no interest in trying to belong in hers.

"And that," he muttered darkly, "is that."

Nodding sharply, he pushed away from the window, stalked over to his duffel and grabbed a red T-shirt with the USMC emblem emblazoned across the front. Yanking it on, he shoved his arms through the sleeves, pushed the tail of the shirt into the waistband of his jeans and headed for the door.

Now that he'd made up his mind, all that was left was to tell Lisa. He owed her that. He owed *himself* that.

He'd go see her right now. Tell her to her face that he was leaving. No doubt she'd agree. Hell, she'd probably been thinking about this all night, too. Now that she was back where she belonged, he was sure she'd come to the same conclusions he had. So it was best to get this whole thing over with and behind them as quickly as possible. Of course, he'd call in a couple of weeks to check out the pregnancy threat. But God willing there would be no baby and they could simply fade from each other's lives.

And maybe in a few dozen years he'd be able to look back on his time with her and not suffer the ache that pounded through him with every beat of his heart.

Travis grabbed the brass knob and gave it a vicious twist. He pulled the room door open and instantly forgot every last one of his well-intentioned plans. Instead he stared into a pair of lake-blue eyes and felt himself drowning in them.

"Hello, Travis," she said, her voice skating along his spine.

And just like that, the roller-coaster ride that was Lisa Chambers, took off again.

Ten

One look into his eyes was all it took. Her knees wobbled and her stomach pitched and rolled. Lisa took a long, deep breath and hoped for balance. It didn't come. Just looking at him was enough to turn her insides to oatmeal.

"What are you doing here?" he asked, and his voice sounded a shade less than welcoming, despite the gleam in his eyes as he looked at her.

She swallowed back her disappointment. Somehow she'd half expected him to sweep her up into a romantic embrace and kiss her the way he had at the oasis. But his stony expression told her that was a vain hope. It was all right, though. Because no matter what he said, she felt his desire for her shimmering in the air between them. He couldn't disguise it any more than she could. And that was something to hang on to.

"Well, it's nice to see you, too." Without waiting for an invitation—because heaven knew it might not be forthcoming—Lisa slipped past him and into the room. She heard him close the door behind her and, just for a moment, she indulged another hope that he'd come up behind her, wrap his arms around her middle and pull her flush up against him. She wanted to feel his warm, solid strength again. Needed to recapture the sensations she'd experienced all too briefly in that faraway desert.

But naturally none of that actually happened.

"I was just coming to see you," he said.

She flinched at the distance in his voice. Ordinarily those would have been good words. But said in that tone, Lisa was sure that if she let him keep talking, she wouldn't like what he had to say.

"Well then," she spoke up quickly, filling the brief silence before he could. "This is what I call good timing."

"Lisa—"

"Travis…" She turned around quickly to face him and, for the space of a single heartbeat, lost herself in the warmth of his gaze. Yet, as tempting as it was to stay lost, she saw in the tension of his stance that he was already preparing himself to say goodbye. And she couldn't let him do that. "I came to take you sight-seeing."

He frowned. Obviously, he hadn't been expecting that. Slowly he folded his arms across his impossibly broad chest. "Sight-seeing?"

For a moment or two she faltered. She should have thought of this. He was a Marine, for Pete's sake. He might have been in D.C. any number of times. Funny, this had seemed like such a good idea a couple of hours ago. Now, she felt...foolish. So just to make things worse, her brain shut down and her mouth took over. "I thought you might like to see some of Washington while you're here. Unless you've been here before, of course." Great, she thought absently as she watched her hands waving about, keeping time with the flood of words. Now she *looked* foolish, too. "Because you know, if you have been here before, then you probably aren't interested. But if you haven't, you really should see some of the city, and I could show you because I've lived here my whole life and—" She finally ran out of breath, thank heaven. Now if only the floor would open up beneath her so she could fall into a black hole.

When she stopped talking, a long minute of strained silence ticked past. Lisa kept her gaze locked with his, as if she could will him into agreeing. And even as she tried, a part of her recognized that if Travis Hawks didn't want to do something, he couldn't be intimidated into it. Wasn't that one of the things she admired about him?

Most of her life the men she met were all eager to do whatever she asked, in hopes of getting in good with her father. Travis, though, couldn't care less who her father was and had more than once voiced his low opinion of "spoiled princesses." Which was why, she told herself, his opinion of her mattered so much.

He reached up and moved both hands along the sides of his head. Lisa watched the play of muscles beneath his faded T-shirt. Her mouth went dry, and a warm curl of something achy and delicious settled low in her belly. Really, he was the most amazing man.

"I was coming to see you," he said, his voice rumbling through the silence like an out-of-control freight train, "to say goodbye."

She winced at the jab of pain those words caused. And the warmth she'd felt only moments ago turned to ice. He was leaving? Already?

"Travis—"

"No, let me say this," he said, stepping close enough that she would have sworn she could hear his heartbeat thundering in time with her own.

"Whatever this is between us? It's no good. You know that, right?"

"No, I don't."

"Damn it, Lisa…"

"Damn it, yourself," she said quickly, letting the words tumble from her mouth in a rushed attempt to head him off at the pass, so to speak. "There's something *magical* between us, Travis, and you know it. We shouldn't waste it. We should be enjoying it."

"It isn't real," he argued and another quick slash of pain shot through her. "It was the danger. The fear. The whole experience of being out in that desert together. It was just circumstance, Lisa."

"No. I don't believe that, and I don't think you do, either." What had happened so briefly between Travis and her had been the most real thing in her life. And she wouldn't let him throw it away so easily.

His features went, if possible, even stonier. If she hadn't known better, she would have thought he was a statue, carved from unforgiving granite.

"What I believe," he said, "is that my world and yours just don't mix."

"They don't have to."

"Yeah, they do. Or they'll collide, and the crash will be something spectacular."

"So to avoid that, you'll run."

He stiffened, and she gave herself a mental point for scoring a direct hit.

"I'm not running."

She glanced at his sneaker clad feet and snorted a short laugh. "Heck, Travis. You've even got your track shoes on to make a little extra time."

"I'm trying to do what's right."

"You're wrong."

"I don't think so."

"And what about me maybe being pregnant?" She had to throw that one in. Lisa still didn't believe that she would prove to be pregnant. After all, one time was one time and what were the odds? She'd probably have a better chance at winning the lottery. Yet she was running out of ammunition and the war wasn't over yet. "What happened to your vow to stay close until we knew?"

He scowled at her, and she knew she had him. Scraping one hand across his jaw, he inhaled sharply and blew out the air in a rush of exasperation. "I'll call you in a couple of weeks and—"

"I won't answer the phone."

"Damn it."

"If you want an answer to that question, Travis," she said, playing her last card, "you'll have to stick around long enough to find out."

"When will you know?"

She shrugged as if she wasn't sure, when in reality, she knew very well that she'd find out one way or the other by the end of the week.

"Why are you doing this?" he asked.

"Why are you *not?*"

"I'm trying to do what's right."

"So am I," she told him and looked up into his eyes.

He grabbed her shoulders, and she felt the hot, strong imprint of each of his fingertips as if he were branding her skin right through the silk of her blouse. Tendrils of excitement and desire spiraled through her body, at direct odds with the near panic rising up in her brain.

"You're crazy, you know that?"

"I can live with that," Lisa said softly, smiling up at him. She'd won. She saw the surrender in his eyes, felt it in his touch. He'd be staying. For a while, at least. And somehow, in the time he was here, she'd have to convince him that they belonged together.

"You're so beautiful."

Lisa blinked. "What?"

"Beautiful," he repeated, and shifted his gaze over her features slowly, lovingly.

Lisa's stomach jittered, and a flush of heat raced through her bloodstream. "I am?"

"Oh, yeah," he said, one dark eyebrow lifting. "And you know it."

All right, so she'd primped a little before coming to see him. What woman wouldn't? After all, she hadn't exactly looked her best out in the desert. Lisa ran the flat of her hands down the front of her charcoal-gray slacks, then fidgeted with the gold chain belt at her waist. Her pale-pink silk blouse suited her, she knew, with its scooped neck and three-quarter-length sleeves. And the small but elegant diamond heart she wore around her neck had belonged to her mother.

She reached up now to finger it nervously.

He lifted one hand from her shoulder to stroke his fingertips along her cheek and sent shivers skipping giddily through her veins. So fast, she thought. So incredibly fast. She'd hardly known him a week, and yet it felt as though her soul had been waiting for him all her life. Lisa didn't understand how this could have happened. And so quickly. Maybe it was the tense situation they'd shared back in the desert. Maybe fear and danger and the need to depend on each other for survival had compressed months of living into a few short days. But it didn't really matter how it had happened. The simple fact was she had absolutely no doubts.

She loved Travis Hawks.

For the next few days Travis spent almost every waking moment with Lisa. And leaving her every night was getting more and more difficult. His body ached to join hers again. His hands itched to touch her, and the taste of her still lingered on his tongue. Desire chewed at his soul until it was all he could do to keep from grabbing her.

And damned if she wasn't enjoying it. He could see it in the way she moved. The way she talked. The way she gave him those long, smoldering glances from beneath lowered eyelids. She touched him all the time. A stroke on the arm, a pat on the cheek. She threaded her arm through his and walked close enough beside him that he swore he felt her body heat pouring into his, making the fires inside burn even brighter.

He was living in a constant state of hunger. His nerves were frayed and his control was slipping. A few more days with her and he'd throw all of his high-minded intentions out the window and toss her onto the nearest bed. All that kept him strong was the knowledge that to make love to her again would only make things worse. As it was, his heart was ragged from the knowledge that he'd be leaving her soon. That their lives would probably never again connect. That these few dwindling days with her were all that he would ever have.

And as he struggled to keep his passion in check, he fed his brain with images of her, so that years from now he'd be able to pull them out, like pictures from a photo album. He told himself that one day he'd be able to remember her without the pain of losing her. But even he didn't believe that.

They traipsed through the Smithsonian, strolled the streets of Williamsburg, Virginia, and visited Ford's theater. They went on a White House tour, saw Congress and the Senate, and now today they were at the mall.

Grassy hills were filled with tourists, snapping pictures of each other and buying stupid souvenirs at the stands plopped along the greenbelt like squatting bugs in the road.

Hand in hand they passed the POW/MIA booth and when his step faltered slightly, Travis felt her hand tighten around his in silent support. Farther along the path, surrounded by leafy trees, stood The Wall. Just a scrape of stone etched into a rise in the ground with thousands of names scrolled across it, the Vietnam memorial was simple yet powerful. At the Korean War memorial, though, Travis stopped dead.

His gaze locked on the small squad of soldiers, frozen in time. Lisa's hand in his was warm, alive and he welcomed her strength as he studied the faces of the statues. Young men, eyes alert for trouble, they moved through a marsh, weapons ready. Behind them a gray granite wall was etched with hundreds of faces, giving the impression of ghosts ready to step out from beyond whatever veil separated them from this world.

Travis's jaw clenched. Every professional soldier felt a kinship with those still missing. Like an empty chair at a dinner table, their absence was never forgotten. Silently he said a brief prayer for the lost men and women who had never come home—then took another moment to be grateful that he had. He looked at Lisa then, standing so close, and found her gaze fixed on him. Understanding and compassion shone in her eyes, and his heart swelled painfully in his chest.

"You're really something, princess," he whispered, knowing it wasn't enough. But how did you find the words to tell a woman how much she meant to you when at the same time you were trying to distance yourself from her?

She leaned into him, her shoulder-length blond hair lifting in the soft wind. "It's not so hard to understand what you would be thinking right now."

"It's this place," he said, tearing his gaze from hers long enough to sweep the surrounding area. "It's good to see it. To see all the people here. To know that no one's been forgotten." It was more, of course. Monuments to the fallen, remembrances of past bravery, made him proud to be who and what he was. And knowing she, too, was proud, touched him.

"You won't be forgotten, either," she said, and

the tone of her voice drew his gaze back to her. "Not by me. Not ever."

Before he could think of a response, she let go of his hand and started walking. Spring sunshine fell across her like a blessing. Her white slacks and red, long-sleeved shirt looked fresh and bright. Her blond hair gleamed in the sunlight, and the sway of her hips tightened his body and stole his breath.

This was nuts and he knew it.

They'd been together for days now. And every night, when he was lying alone in his bed, in that empty hotel room, he told himself to leave town. To get out while he still could. Yet every morning he waited for her, looking forward to his first glimpse of her. How was he going to live without her? How would he face the coming years knowing that he wouldn't be able to look into those eyes of hers, hear her laugh or feel her touch?

He was a damn fool for staying around as long as he had, and it wasn't getting any easier. If he had any sense at all, he'd hop the first plane to Texas, spend some time with the family, then rejoin his squad. Face the next mission.

But even as he thought it, he knew none of that would be enough to help him forget Lisa Chambers.

Two days later Lisa moved through the crowd but kept her gaze on Travis. Her father's house was filled with the rich and mighty, gathered together for a formal dinner party in Travis's honor. Tuxedos, designer gowns and enough jewelry to give a cat burglar a heart attack crowded the room, but she saw only one man. Wearing his dress blue uniform, Travis Hawks stood out from the rest of the people like an eagle in the midst of a flock of pigeons. Though obviously uncomfortable in his surroundings, he stood tall and gorgeous, looking like a poster of For God and Country. While the men around him discussed financial statements and tax shelters, he quietly stole the attention of every female in the room.

And she was no exception. Smiling at the familiar faces she passed, she nodded appropriately at all the right times, mouthed a few pleasantries and all the time concentrated on keeping her heart from breaking. She hadn't been able to reach him. Despite what she knew they shared, Travis was going to leave. She sensed it in him. Knew their time was almost over...and couldn't come up with a plan to stop him.

"Oh, Lisa," a female voice cooed, "you simply *must* tell me everything about that gorgeous man."

She glanced at Serena Hathaway, forced a smile and resumed her role as hostess.

Travis didn't know how they all stood it. He'd

never been so bored in his life. These people, standing around pretending to be interested in whatever anyone else was saying, made mingling an art form. He felt as out of place as a thief in church. But Lisa, he told himself, fitted right in here. This was her world, and it couldn't have been explained any more clearly to him.

She looked beautiful, of course, in a forest-green, floor-length dress that clung to her slim figure with a lover's caress. Her hair was swept up on top of her head and held in place by a clip with diamonds. More sparklers winked at her ears, and he was willing to guess the diamond necklace she wore cost more than he'd make in his entire career.

Yep. As much as he hated being here, it was a good thing he'd come. Seeing Lisa in her element, he realized just how far out of his reach she really was. Now maybe he could make his heart believe it.

"Ah, Travis," her father said, coming up behind him and slapping one arm around his shoulder, "you don't mind if I call you Travis, I hope."

"No, sir," he said, and noted that though the man was talking to him, his gaze was shifting past him to others in the room.

"I'd like a word with you in my study."

Nodding, Travis followed him, relieved to have a distraction from his thoughts of Lisa, even if only for a minute. He stepped into a distinctly masculine room filled with bookshelves. Maroon leather chairs crouched before a now-cold fireplace, and crystal bottles of amber liquor glistened from the top of a polished bar. The smell of cigar smoke lingered here, and even as he had that thought, Alan Chambers stepped behind a wide, mahogany desk, lit a cigar and offered one to him.

"No, thank you."

The other man puffed a bit, sighed, then walked over and sat down in one of the chairs, indicating Travis should join him.

He studied his cigar for a second, then said, "I wanted to thank you again personally for everything you did for my daughter."

"Not necessary, sir," Travis told him. "I was just doing my job."

"Of course. But still, it must have been difficult dealing with a woman so..." He let the sentence just hang there, as if he couldn't find the proper word to end it.

Annoyed, Travis supplied, *"Brave?"*

Chambers blinked, then laughed shortly. "Well now, there's a word not often used to describe my little girl."

Irritation shot through him, but he tamped it down. After all, this was Lisa's father.

"Now," the man went on, "I'm the first to admit

that my girl's the woman to call if you want an affair handled correctly. But Lisa? In a desert? No, no. If not for you, well, I wouldn't like to think what might have happened.''

Remembering her tenacity, her sheer will, Travis said firmly, ''She would have found a way to survive.''

The man actually chuckled again. And this time Travis took offense.

''Mr. Chambers, sir, I have to say you don't know a thing about that woman.''

''I beg your pardon?''

''It's *her* pardon you ought to be begging. That's a hell of a woman out there, and she deserves better from her own father.''

''Now see here...''

''No, sir,'' Travis said, standing up, ''I see plenty. I see a man so wrapped up in making his next million he doesn't see what's right under his nose. A daughter to be proud of. To love.''

''Who the hell do you think you are, Marine?''

''I know who I am, Mr. Chambers,'' Travis said through clenched teeth. ''And I know who Lisa is. It's you I can't figure out.''

The older man rose from his chair, but was still forced to look up to meet Travis's gaze. Anger flashed briefly in Alan Chambers's eyes. ''It's been a long time since anyone's spoken to me like that.''

"Then maybe it's time, sir," Travis said, refusing to back down on this one. He'd seen Lisa at her worst, and he was willing to bet that she'd done a damn sight better in that desert than her father would have in the same situation. "Lisa's strong and capable and smart."

"Is that right?"

"Damn straight. I'm not saying she's perfect. She's got a hard head and a temper to match. But she made me proud out in that desert. And you should be proud of her, too."

"Interesting."

"Yeah?"

"You're in love with my daughter, aren't you?"

Stunned, Travis stared at the man as if he was suddenly speaking Greek. "What?"

"Answer the question, Travis," Lisa said from the doorway.

Both men spun around to face her as she slipped through the door and closed it behind her.

"How long have you been there?" Travis demanded.

"Long enough to know I want to hear you answer my father's question."

He looked from Lisa to her father and back again. Emotions churned inside him, but he'd be damned if he'd let himself be cornered. Those blue eyes of hers locked on him, and he felt the slam of their punch right down to his bones. But he couldn't give her what she wanted.

If nothing else, being in this house tonight had taught him that much.

''The answer's no, Lisa,'' he said softly, nearly choking on the lie.

Eleven

Lisa flinched as if he'd struck her. Pain blossomed inside her and spread on a slow moving tide of misery. Amazing how much power one small word could carry. Her gaze locked with his, she fought to draw breath. She stared into his eyes, and even from across the room she saw regret shimmering in those brown depths.

"You're lying," she whispered, her voice breaking on the words.

His features twisted briefly. "Lisa—"

"Why are you lying?" she asked, not really expecting an answer. He didn't disappoint her. He didn't say anything, simply stared at her through eyes that looked as pained as she felt.

"Honey," her father spoke up, and she jumped, startled. She'd almost forgotten he was in the room. And frankly she didn't care. All that mattered at the moment was Travis and making him admit that he cared for her. She couldn't be wrong about this. She couldn't be. She'd felt the passion in him. The tenderness. It was more than desire between them and they both knew it.

"Let him go," her father said. "Don't make another mistake. Five engagements are enough for anyone."

"Five?"

She stiffened and met Travis's stunned gaze squarely. She probably should have told him about those engagements herself. "Yes, five." Slanting a quick glance at her father, she frowned at him, then looked back at the man still watching her. "I tried," she said, hoping to explain to him what she'd only recently discovered herself. "Tried to be what everyone expected me to be. But they were no different than my father."

"Excuse me?" The older man blurted.

She ignored him, focusing her gaze on Travis. Willing him to understand. "They wanted me for a decoration. An asset at parties. They didn't care who I was or what I thought. Not really. They saw the

Chambers name and that was enough for them.'' She took a step closer. "Don't you see, Travis? I wanted, needed to be more. And with you…I am."

"Five broken engagements are nothing to be proud of," her father said tightly.

She winced, but before she could speak in her own defense, Travis turned on the man.

"You're her father, for God's sake. Shouldn't you be on *her* side?"

"I am," the man insisted.

"Then God help your enemies," Travis said bluntly. "Don't you think it's better that she had five broken engagements rather than five divorces? Can't you be proud of her for recognizing a mistake and taking steps to correct it?"

Lisa's heart filled until she wouldn't have been surprised to see it fly from her chest. She'd never been defended so nobly. She'd never seen anyone stand up to her father. And watching Travis in action made her love him all the more.

"Sergeant, you are out of line," her father muttered.

"Mr. Chambers, you're probably right. So to remedy that, I'll be leaving."

"Don't go."

He looked at her. "It's no good, Lisa. It wouldn't work."

"Isn't it worth a try?" she demanded, ignoring her father's blustering.

Travis stalked across the room in a few long strides and paused when he reached her side. Lifting one of his hands, he touched her cheek and gave her a half smile that tugged at the corners of her heart. "Trying wouldn't change the facts." Shaking his head, he said softly, "Goodbye, princess."

And then he was gone.

When the door was closed again, her father spoke up. "You're better off without him."

"Better?" Head pounding, heart aching, her eyes swimming with tears, she whirled around to face the man who had never seen the real her. "Better how, Dad? Is it better for me to stay here in this house, running your life, arranging your parties?" She lifted the hem of her dress and marched across the room, not stopping until she was within arm's reach of him. "What exactly is that better than? Having my own life? A husband? A family?" She sucked in a gulp of air and tried to ease the ache inside her. But it was too big. Too all encompassing to be shoved aside. Lisa reached up and rubbed away a solitary tear. She didn't have time to cry. Didn't have the luxury of indulging a bout of self-pity.

Looking up at her father, she studied his perplexed expression and realized that she hadn't been entirely fair to him, either. After all, if she'd never stood up and demanded that he take notice of her...the *real* her...then how could she be angry that he hadn't?

"This isn't all your fault, Dad," she said, nodding to herself. "I gave up my dreams because it was easier to be what you needed me to be."

"Your dreams? You mean teaching?"

"Yes," she said, reaching out to lay one hand on her father's arm.

"You couldn't have earned a decent living on a teacher's salary," he reminded her.

She smiled and shook her head. "That all depends on what your idea of decent is, doesn't it?" She looked up at him and silently admitted that she'd blamed him too long for the things that had gone wrong in her life. If she wanted a new start, a new life, then she would have to go out and make it on her own. "I love you, Dad," she said, watching him closely enough that she caught the flicker of emotion in his eyes and was pleased. "But I can't be just your daughter anymore. I have to find a place for myself."

He studied the ash tip of his cigar for a moment or two, then asked, "With him?"

"Oh, yes."

"Humph. Well, the man's got guts, I give him that."

"Yes, he does."

"Stood right up to me and called me on my own carpet."

"I know." She smiled. "Pretty impressive, huh?"

"Yes," he said, reaching for her and pulling her close for a hug. "But not as impressive as my daughter."

Lisa closed her eyes, wrapped her arms around his middle and hung on, savoring the sweetness of this one perfect moment. Amazing what a little honesty could do for a person.

"I do love you, honey," he said, his voice soft as a caress. "I always have."

"I know that, Dad." But, oh, how good it was to hear the words.

He gave her a pat, cleared his throat, then leaned back to look down at her. "So. Just how do you plan on convincing that man to see things your way?"

Oh, she had some very definite ideas on that. But they weren't plans she felt comfortable sharing with her father. So rather than go into specifics, all she said was, "Trust me, Dad. I'll make him an offer he can't refuse."

The ache in his chest would go away eventually. Twenty or thirty years ought to take care of it. Travis scowled at the man in the mirror and snatched up his shaving kit. Stomping back into the bedroom, he shoved the kit into his duffel, then tossed the whole bag onto the nearest chair. It hit with a thud, which did nothing to ease the tension clawing at his insides.

"Nice job, Travis. Tell her father off, then leave her to deal with the mess." Yeah, he'd handled that really well. Shaking his head in disgust, he paced the room like a prisoner on death row looking for a chink in his cage.

But there wasn't one.

He kept seeing her face when he'd said goodbye.

Pain. It had shimmered over her, through her and then reached its grasping hands out for him. The bite of her pain was still stronger than his. His back teeth ground together, he shook his head in an attempt to dislodge that last portrait of her, and walked to the window. Throwing it open, he leaned into the wind, feeling its full force.

She'd get over it, he told himself firmly. Hadn't she been engaged *five* times already? *Yes,* a voice inside whispered. But then it reminded him that she'd been a virgin until that sun-filled morning with him at the oasis. She'd waited. For him. For love. Just as she would wait again.

And one day…she'd find love again. Then someone else would touch her as Travis had. Someone else would swallow her gasps and lose himself in her eyes. And that knowledge ripped what was left of his heart from his chest.

He closed his eyes against the starry sky and saw her in memory, her naked body dappled with the shade of the palm trees. His body tightened, his mind drifted back and he could almost feel her skin beneath his hands. The warm smoothness of her. The silky slide of his callused palms across her flesh. His mouth went dry, and he knew that if he tried, he could still taste her on his lips.

But why up the torture level? He scrubbed both hands across his face as if he could somehow wipe away his thoughts.

A knock on the door brought him lurching around to glare at the intrusion. Vowing to get rid of whoever was standing on the other side of that door, he stalked across the room, yanked it open and snarled, "What?"

"Ah, you've missed me," Lisa said, and pushed past him into the room.

His breath caught hard in his chest like a cold ball of lead. "Go home, Lisa."

"What would you say if I said I *was* home?"

"I'd say you're nuts. This is a hotel."

"I meant, being here with you."

"I know what you meant and you're wrong."

"Am I?" She turned around to look at him.

She'd changed out of that party dress, but this

outfit was just as alluring. A sleeveless top scooped low at the neck and clung to her breasts before skimming her rib cage and disappearing beneath the waist of her skirt. And the hem of that short, tight black skirt stopped at midthigh, exposing her shapely, stocking-clad legs to full advantage.

She wore high, spindly heels that made him wonder how she could keep her balance, and when she cocked her right hip, he watched the muscles in her legs shift with mouthwatering fascination.

Oh, he was in for a hard time now.

Still, he called on years of Marine training to shut off his emotions and focus on the job at hand. And that job was getting her the hell out of his room before he did something stupid like make love to her again.

"Yeah," he said tightly, "you're wrong. You don't belong with me. So, do us both a favor and go home. Find yourself fiancé number six somewhere else."

She blanched, and he gave himself a solid mental kick. But being kind wasn't going to get rid of her, and damn it, she *had* to go.

"I thought you understood. About my engagements," she said. "You told my father—"

"I do understand," he said, despite his better judgment. He wouldn't hurt her any more than he absolutely had to. "But you have to understand something, too. I can't be who you want me to be."

"And who's that?" she asked, folding her arms beneath her breasts and pushing them up until he saw the tops of them rising just above that scoop-necked blouse.

He swallowed hard. "The man you need. A man who's comfortable at a party like the one tonight."

"If that's what I wanted, I would have married one of those five fiancés."

True, he told himself, but couldn't take comfort from it. Because it changed nothing. It fixed nothing.

"We're too different, Lisa."

"No, we're not."

"Hell, you could put my family's house inside your father's and still have room for the garage."

"Do you think I care about that?"

"*I* care."

"Then you're an idiot."

"So find yourself someone who's not."

"I don't want anyone else."

"Damn it, Lisa, don't make this harder than it has to be."

"Oh," she said, locking her gaze with his, "I'm going to make it a lot harder." Then, before he knew it, she was peeling that blouse up, up and off.

His heart hammered in his chest. His body went on full alert. "What do you think you're doing?"

"I think," she said, "I'm seducing you."

Next came the bra. She undid the front clasp, and his mouth went dry as she shrugged out of the lemon-yellow silk, baring her breasts to him. Her nipples peaked, and all he could think of was tasting them, suckling them, drawing them deeper and deeper into his mouth until she was writhing beneath him, begging him for the release only he could give her.

But he couldn't. *Could* he?

She reached around to her back, slid the zipper on her skirt down, then let the damn thing fall to the floor. His heart stopped.

Flat-out stopped.

She wasn't wearing underwear, heaven help him. Just a slim black garter belt that rode her hips, slid low across her abdomen and held up the stockings that clung to her upper thighs.

Travis felt sweat break out on his forehead. He reached up, rubbed one hand across the back of his neck and reminded himself to breathe. But he knew if he could just get his hands on her, he wouldn't even need to breathe. Lisa. All he needed was Lisa. Damn it. His entire body seemed to be pulsing to a throbbing need that was crouched low inside him, waiting to pounce. When he thought he could speak again, he lifted his gaze to hers and lied as best he could. "This isn't working."

She smiled, a slow, knowing smile that women have been giving men for centuries. Then her gaze dropped to his crotch. "Seems to be working fine."

Caught by his own body's reaction to her. He exhaled heavily, narrowed his gaze on her and said, "Think you're pretty smart, don't you?"

"Hmm." She planted her hands at her hips and—the only word for it—sashayed toward him. Then she reached out with one hand and let her fingertips slide down his chest, scraping against the fabric of his T-shirt. "As a matter of fact, yes. I guess I do."

He could smell her. Her perfume swam in his head until his thoughts were nothing but a blur of need and hunger. He'd have to be a dead man not to respond to her. And he sure as hell wasn't dead. One more night, he thought. One more night with her. Was that so much to ask?

Travis grabbed her. One arm snaking out to wrap around her waist, he yanked her to him and held her tight against him.

"Travis…"

"I want you bad," he muttered, sliding one hand up her body to cup one breast. His thumb and forefinger tweaked her nipple, and when she shivered, he felt as though he'd just been awarded a medal.

"You can have me," she said, tipping her head back to look him dead in the eye. "That's what I've been trying to tell you. We can have each other. We can have it all.''

"Don't want it all," he murmured, lowering his head to hers. "Just want you."

And then he kissed her and felt everything else fall away. Nothing, no one, was more important than this moment. She wrapped her arms around his neck and clung to him. And still it wasn't enough. He needed to feel her. Be a part of her. Slide himself so deeply into her that even apart they would be together. Dropping his hands to her bottom, he lifted her, and she wound her legs around his middle.

Hunger roared inside him, demanding to be fed and he surrendered to it. Thoughts, desires, emotions clamored in his brain but all he could focus on was the feel of her. He slid one hand farther along her body and touched her damp heat.

She jolted in his grasp, but he held her tightly. Taking her mouth with his, he savored the taste of her, the glory of her, while his hands explored her secrets and drove her along the high road to passion. She twisted in his grasp, moving into his touch, trying to take more of him inside her.

His tongue entwined with hers, tasting, taking, giving. She moaned gently and broke the kiss, letting her head fall back, allowing him access to her throat. She arched into him, pressing her breasts to his chest, moving her hips in time with his touch and sighing when his teeth nipped at the base of her neck.

"I love you, Travis," she whispered, and the words shot into his heart with the accuracy of a sniper's bullet.

Breathing hard, he lifted his head, looked directly into her eyes and admitted, "I love you, Lisa. Too damn much."

She smiled. "It's never enough, Travis. I'll never have enough of you. Be with me. Be inside me."

Man, he wanted that more than anything, but he still didn't have any protection. But then why should he? He'd planned on being all noble.

As if she could read his mind, she smiled, reared back in his arms and slowly, tauntingly, slid one hand down her body. Like a lover, she touched herself, skimming her fingertips across her breasts, along her rib cage, to the edge of that garter belt.

His throat closed up just watching. "What're you…"

She slipped her fingertips beneath the black lace belt and when she pulled them free, she was holding two small, foil packages.

His heartbeat thundered. "Two, huh? You were pretty sure of yourself."

"Uh-uh," she said, shaking her head. "Sure of you."

He nodded, grabbed the condoms from her and

then dropped her unceremoniously onto the bed. Laughing, she bounced on the mattress and watched him as he quickly stripped off his clothes. Then he ripped open the small package, fit the condom to himself and joined her.

Lisa smiled up at him and said, "Give me a minute and I'll get these heels and stockings off."

"Leave 'em on," he ordered, and dipped his head to take first one nipple then the other into his mouth.

She cried out and moved into him, offering herself up to his ministrations. Pleasure, deep, soul-satisfying pleasure rushed through her, and she sighed and gave in to it. Her mind blanked out. All she could think of, all she could feel, was Travis. Now. Always. She couldn't lose him. Not after this. Not when they were so clearly meant for each other.

He touched her, dipping one finger into her heat, and Lisa's hips lifted. That slow, deep tickle built within and she fostered it, moving into his touch, trailing her hands up and down his back. She wanted him. Needed him.

His thumb brushed an especially sensitive spot, and her legs fell open. Eagerness rushed through her blood and fed the desire already nearly choking her. His mouth. His hands. He suckled her and she gasped, feeling the drawing sensation right down to the soles of her feet. Too much, her brain shouted, but her body refused the warning. It would never be too much. Never. Her lungs heaved for air that wouldn't come. Her blood pumped through her veins, liquid fire.

"Travis," she said, lifting her hips higher off the bed, "I need...I need you. Now."

"Me, too, baby," he said, lifting his head long enough to kiss her firmly. Then he moved to kneel between her legs, and she watched as he stroked her center. A quickening started low in her belly. A flutter of expectation. A rush of urgency. When the first eruption began, he pushed himself inside her and she clung to him, wrapping her legs around his hips, pulling him deeper, closer.

He whispered her name, and it sounded like a prayer.

She looked up into his eyes and welcomed his kiss that joined them completely. His hands captured hers, fingers locking, gripping.

And then they were tumbling off the edge of a cliff, together.

Twelve

"**W**hat do you mean you're still leaving?"

Travis sat up and looked at her. "This didn't change anything, Lisa."

Pain blended with fury. Just a half hour ago this man had held her, made love to her and even, for one brief moment, actually admitted his love for her. Now *this?* Lisa swung her hair back out of her eyes, pushed herself up and, clutching the sheet to her chest, demanded, "Then what will, Travis?"

He shook his head and stood up. Lisa couldn't take her gaze off him. In the lamplight pooling around him, his broad shoulders, muscular back and narrow hips shone golden, as if he were an impossibly gorgeous sculpture. But then he moved, shattering the image, and the look on his face when he turned toward her was too full of apology to be anything but real.

"That's the trouble. Nothing will."

"I don't accept that." She wouldn't. Couldn't. Darn it, she hadn't waited for love this long just to find it, then have it snatched away.

"You have to," he said, grabbing up his pants from the floor. Tugging them on, he glanced at her. "Hell, princess, you saw it yourself tonight."

"What do you mean?" She pushed one hand through her hair, angrily shoving it out of her way.

"That party. Those people." He threw his hands up and laughed, a short, raspy sound that held no humor. "I mean, your father's got an actual *ballroom* in his house."

"*His* house," she reminded him quickly. "Not mine."

"Doesn't matter," he said. "Don't you get it? That's what you're used to." He laughed again and shook his head. "I'd never be able to give you marble floors and private jets and chefs. I can't give you chauffeurs and designer dresses." He looked at her for a long minute, then added, "And I won't offer you less."

"You think I care about any of that?"

"*I* care. That's the point."

Panic reared its ugly head. All her life her father's money had mattered. Everyone she'd ever met had been suspect. Did they want to know her for herself or for the Chambers name and fortune? Now, it was coming down to the money again. Only, this time the man she loved *didn't* want her because of the money.

"But none of that matters to me, Travis. I'm not interested in what you *can't* give me." She clambered off the bed, dragging the sheet with her and wrapping it around her naked body like a makeshift toga. Clutching it to her breasts with one hand, she reached out with the other and laid it flat on his chest. She concentrated briefly on the steady pound of his heart beneath her palm, then said, "I just want to know if you love me."

He caught her hand in his and squeezed it gently. Then, lifting it, he kissed her knuckles before releasing her again. Taking a step back from her, almost as if he didn't trust himself to be too close, he said, "Yes, Lisa. I love you."

Hope sparked to life in her heart, then winked out again a moment later when he kept talking.

"But I'm not going to ask you to marry me."

She opened her mouth to argue, but he cut her off.

"Because," he said, his gaze locked with hers,

"one of these days you'd regret giving up everything you've ever known for the kind of life you'd have as a Marine wife."

This couldn't be happening.

He *loved* her.

He'd admitted it.

And still she was going to lose him?

No. She wouldn't let her father's fortune be the deciding factor in her—their—happiness. She wouldn't let this be the end. "Travis—"

"I've already got a flight out. I leave tomorrow." The words tasted dry and bitter, but he forced himself to say them. This was for the best, he told himself. For both of them.

He didn't want to wake up one morning a few years from now and see regret in her eyes. Better he deal with the pain now, than wait until they had a few children. Children.

Baby.

His gaze shot straight to her eyes. "I'll call you in a few days."

"Why?"

"To see if—"

"Oh, yes," she said, and her voice sounded wounded, distant. "You have to do the right thing, don't you? Can't have a pesky pregnancy turning up without you knowing about it."

"Lisa…"

"What if I am pregnant?" she asked, lifting her chin into that defiant tilt he'd come to know so well in the desert. "What then, Travis?"

He didn't know. He just hoped to God she wouldn't be. Then neither of them would be forced into a marriage that could only end badly. It tore at him to think of leaving her...of never seeing her again. But what else could he do?

"We'll talk about that if and when it happens," he said.

"An answer for everything." She brushed past him, headed for the clothes she'd discarded such a short time ago.

He watched her as she let the sheet drop, and felt the hard, solid punch of desire again when he got another eyeful of her in that garter belt. But desire would die eventually if it was smothered by a blanket of resentment. And damn it, she *would* resent him. Sooner or later she would start thinking about what she could have had if she hadn't fallen in love with a Marine.

Two weeks ago he hadn't known she existed. Now the thought of living without her was almost enough to kill him. Who would have guessed that love could strike so quickly, so completely?

In just a few minutes she was dressed and facing him. Her expression was frozen. Only her eyes were alive and they glimmered with a pain he knew he'd caused. Travis fought down the urge to grab her and crush her to him. His arms ached, and an empty sensation opened up around his heart. The years ahead of him stretched out for an eternity that he knew would be filled with memories of her and the haunting images of what might have been.

"I'm not going to argue with you about this any longer, Travis," she said, and he heard goodbye in that short speech.

A part of him wanted her to argue. To find a way to talk him out of this decision. Yet a small, rational corner of his mind was grateful that she'd accepted it. Because her not fighting the inevitable would make this so much easier. Even though it killed him to know that she, too, was going to walk away.

"I thought you were different," she said. "I thought that this time it would be about me. Not my father's money—*me*."

That hit him hard. "I don't give a good damn about your father's money."

"Wrong, Travis. That's all you care about." She walked across the room and stopped alongside him. Looking up into his eyes, she shook her head, and when she spoke again, her tone held an iciness he'd never heard from her before. "When we should be celebrating our love, we're saying goodbye. Why? Because my *father* has money."

He hissed in a breath through clenched teeth. "I'm doing this for you, Lisa."

"Uh-huh. Tell yourself that on those cold, lonely nights in your future, Travis. Maybe it'll help."

Then she left, quietly closing the door behind her. Silence crowded in around him. The shadows in the corners seemed to reach out for him, as if they were going to drag him deeper into the darkness. And then he knew. Nothing could help him through all the lonely nights to come.

Through delays and layovers and more delays, Travis's military transport flight took him hours longer than it would have, had he flown on a regular airline. And through it all his brain worked, taunting him, punishing him. Images of Lisa stayed with him, and he knew this was just the beginning. She'd never be out of his heart. His soul. Walking away from her had been like taking a knife and hacking off a limb. The ache went bone deep. Not even stepping out of the plane and into the hot Texas wind was enough to lighten the black mood riding him.

He called home to alert the family that he was on his way. Then he got a ride to the nearest car rental agency and within an hour he was driving down the road, headed home. But for the first time in his life, he didn't want to be there. His heart was in D.C.— and he never should have left.

His hands tightened on the wheel and squeezed. All he could think about was Lisa. Holding her, loving her, losing her. How she'd looked at him through wounded eyes.

"Damn it." He let go of the wheel just long enough to slam his fist against it. "I'm an idiot." That fact went down hard. But it was so true he couldn't deny it any longer. She'd risked everything. She was willing to give up everything. For *him*. And he'd looked her dead in the eye and told her it wasn't enough. He squeezed that steering wheel tightly enough to snap it in two. "Hell," he muttered, "I'm lucky she didn't shoot me."

But then she hadn't had to. The pain in her eyes had stabbed at him, doing far more damage than any weapon could have done. And there was only one cure for it. As he realized what he had to do—what he *needed* to do, a sense of urgency filled him. His heartbeat accelerated. His breathing quickened. Now all he had to do was convince Lisa.

Pulling into the drive, he listened to the scrape and rustle of the gravel beneath the tires, then parked the rental car behind his brother's truck. Judging by the three other cars clustered in the drive, the whole family had gathered to say hello. Well, he thought, scrambling out of the car, they'd just have to wait their turn. First things first.

Grabbing his duffel out of the back seat, he

headed for the two-story Victorian where he'd grown up. Sunshine yellow with sage-green trim, the old place looked familiar, comfortable. It had withstood tornadoes, brush fires and more than a hundred years of hard living—not to mention him and his brothers.

The door flew open when he was halfway across the yard, and a grin he couldn't stop creased his face as he watched his sister race down the steps toward him. He dropped his bag and grabbed her up into a tight hug.

"Sarah, it's good to see you," he said as he swung her around before plopping her back onto her feet. Shifting his gaze to the house again, he asked, "Where's Mom?"

"Inside," she said, smiling. "Along with everybody else."

"Good. That's good." He nodded, grabbed up his duffel bag out of the back seat, then dropped one arm around his sister's shoulders. "I've got something to tell all of you."

"Yeah?" she asked, tipping her head back to look up at him. "What's that?"

"Not yet," he said, shaking his head. "First I have to make a phone call."

"Interesting."

"You have no idea." Already thinking ahead, Travis tried to come up with just the right words, just the right apologies that would convince Lisa to give him another chance. And if she wouldn't take his call, then he'd just fly back to D.C. and camp out on her father's doorstep until she *had* to talk to him.

"So who is she?"

"How do you know it's a she?"

"Oh, please." Sarah laughed and broke away from him, taking the five steps to the porch at a run.

His older brother, John, appeared in the doorway and held the screen door open for him. Grabbing the duffel, he said, "Been a while, little brother."

"Too long." He shook his brother's hand, then grinned as Lucas stepped into the hall, fists up, bobbing and weaving on the balls of his feet.

"Okay, Travis, I've been practicing, and this time I'm gonna win."

"Later." Ignoring his brothers and sister, he walked on into the living room, looking for his mother. God, it felt good to be back here. Here, where nothing changed. Where family was everything. And here is where he wanted Lisa.

"Hello, honey," his mother said and walked across the polished wood floor to collect a hug.

"Hi, Mom." His arms went around her, lifting her clean off the floor until she squealed, slapped his shoulders and demanded to be set down.

Her short, black hair was windswept and tousled.

Her sharp, brown gaze locked on him even as she smiled and shook her head. "You're too thin. But I can take care of that."

"I've been looking forward to your cooking for weeks," he said. "And as soon as I make a phone call, I'll be ready for everything you've got."

"A phone call? To whom?"

"Lisa. Mom, you're gonna love her. She's funny and smart and way too good for me."

"Is that right?"

"Oh, yeah." He shoved one hand across the top of his head and moved to the phone. "Now all I have to do is convince her that I love her."

He picked up the receiver as his mother said, "Why don't you go on and get something to eat first?"

"This can't wait," he told her with a grin, but took a long deep breath, hoping for the scent of his mother's special pot roast. That grin dissolved into a thoughtful scowl. He could have sworn he smelled Lisa's perfume. That mingled scent of citrus and flowers seemed to be everywhere, now that he noticed. But that wasn't possible—so clearly, he was way further gone than even he'd thought. His mind was conjuring up her scent just to torture him.

Shaking his head, he dialed O and asked for directory assistance. Then he waited.

"What's the matter, Travis?" Sarah asked.

"Nothing."

His sister laughed and his mother warned, "Sarah…"

Lucas and John grinned at him, and Travis had the distinct feeling that everyone here was in on a joke but him. "What's goin' on?" he demanded, and an instant later heard the answer to his question.

"Frances," a too-familiar female voice called from the kitchen, "something's wrong."

"What city please?" a voice in his ear inquired, and slowly he hung up the phone and turned around.

Travis swallowed hard and fought down a rush of expectancy. He shot his mother a look, but she only shrugged, smiled and dropped into a chair. Footsteps tapped against the floorboards, and he watched Lisa hurry down the hall from the kitchen.

She wore faded blue jeans, a denim shirt and sneakers. Her blond hair was in a ponytail that danced with her every step, she had his mother's apron tied around her middle and a wooden spoon in her hand.

He felt as though someone had punched him in the stomach. All the air left his body, and he had to try twice just to say her name. "Lisa?"

She ignored him, staring directly at his mother. "Frances, everything's ruined. The stew's boiling over and the bread's black."

"I'll be right there," his mother assured her as

Lisa whirled around and marched back down the hall. When she was gone, Frances looked up at her son. "I could go help…unless, of course, *you'd* like to offer your services instead."

With his family's laughter bursting out around him, Travis stalked down the short hallway, pushed through the swinging door and stepped into the large, square, pale-blue kitchen. He wasn't crazy. She really was there. In his house. At the stove. And she wasn't looking at him.

Grabbing her, he turned her around, keeping both hands at her shoulders. Those blue eyes of hers stared up at him, and he'd never been so glad to see anyone in his life. But he fought down the elation streaking through him to get a few answers first.

"What are you doing here?" he demanded.

"At the moment," she said, with a disgusted glance at the stove behind her, "burning dinner. But I'll learn."

"That's not what I meant."

"I know." Lisa stared up at him and tried to keep her heart from bursting right out of her chest. It hadn't been difficult to decide how to handle this. The moment she'd left him in that hotel room, she'd gone home, packed a bag and commandeered her father's jet for a ride to Texas.

His family had welcomed her, and she'd kept herself busy, telling herself she'd done the right thing.

She'd known that the only way to fight Travis's stubbornness was to ignore it. But ever since she'd arrived, doubts had plagued her. What if he'd only been being kind before? What if he'd claimed to love her as a way to ease dumping her? What if she'd made a colossal fool of herself and now was facing humiliation in front of his family?

Now, though, staring up into those chocolate-brown eyes, she saw everything she'd hoped to see and knew she'd done the right thing. She felt the almost electrical charge of warmth skittering through her from his hands directly down to her bones. He loved her.

So, keeping her voice as steady as she could, she took the plunge and said simply, "I came to marry you."

"I don't recall asking," he said, but a shimmer of light in his dark eyes gave her the courage to keep going.

"No, you didn't," she said, lifting both hands to lay her palms on his chest. His heartbeat thundered, and she felt her own quickening to beat in time. "Because you're a hardheaded man."

"I want to do right by you."

"Then marry me."

A muscle in his jaw twitched, then his features cleared and darkened again in an instant. "Are you—"

She had to think about that for a minute, then realized exactly what he was asking. "I don't know," she said, knowing that this was definitely the time for honesty. "But this isn't about a baby. This is about us."

"Yeah, it is."

"Good. We agree."

He shook his head, his gaze moving over her face like a warm caress. "I'm damn glad to see you, princess," he admitted, then added, "in fact, I was just trying to call your father's house to tell you I was going to come back to collect you."

"You were?"

"Oh, yeah." He reached up and cupped her cheek in his palm. "You're too deep inside me, Lisa. You're a part of me. I can't lose you."

She sucked in a gulp of air and blew it out again in a rush. "You won't lose me. I love you."

"I love you, too, princess. But are you sure about what you're doing here? I'm a Marine. That's all I've ever wanted to be. I'm no stockbroker."

She actually laughed and, oh, it felt good. "I don't want help with my portfolio." Fisting her hands in his T-shirt, she pulled him closer and kept her gaze locked with his as she said, "I want you to marry me because you need me."

"I do."

"You want me."

"I do."

"And you love me."

He smiled—a slow, wicked smile that curled her toes and made sensuous promises she planned to hold him to.

"Oh, yes, ma'am. I do."

"You keep practicing those two little words, all right?"

"I guess I can do that," he said, dropping his hands to her waist and pulling her flush against him.

Sliding her palms up his chest, she wrapped her arms around his neck, looked up at him and said, "You stole my heart, Travis. Out in that desert you claimed it, whether you meant to or not."

He bent his head, resting his forehead against hers, and released a long breath he hadn't known he'd been holding. For the first time since leaving D.C., he felt…whole again. "You can't have your heart back, princess. But you can have mine. It's belonged to you from almost the first moment I laid eyes on you."

With the stew erupting on the stove and black smoke still curling from the oven, Travis kissed his princess. And the moment their lips met, he knew, deep in his soul, that he was finally the richest man in Texas.

* * * * *

Silhouette *Desire*

presents

A brand-new miniseries about the Connellys of Chicago,
a wealthy, powerful American family tied by blood to the
royal family of the island kingdom of Altaria.
They're wealthy, powerful and rocked by
scandal, betrayal…and passion!

Look for a whole year of glamorous and
utterly romantic tales in 2002:

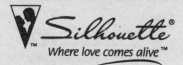

Where love comes alive™

Silhouette Books is proud to present:

Going to the Chapel

**Three brand-new stories
about getting that special man to the altar!**

featuring

USA Today bestselling author

SHARON SALA

It Happened One Night...that Georgia society belle
Harley June Beaumont went to Vegas—and woke up married!
How could she explain her hunk of a husband to
her family back home?

Award-winning author

DIXIE BROWNING

Marrying a Millionaire...was exactly what Grace McCall was
trying to keep her baby sister from doing. Not that Grace had
anything against the groom—it was the groom's arrogant
millionaire uncle who got Grace all hot and bothered!

National bestselling author

STELLA BAGWELL

The Bride's Big Adventure...was escaping her handpicked
fiancé in the arms of a hot-blooded cowboy! And from the
moment Gloria Rhodes said "I do" to her rugged groom, she
dreamed their wedded bliss would never end!

Available in July at your favorite retail outlets!

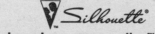

Where Texas society reigns supreme—and appearances are *everything*.

Coming in June 2002
Stroke of Fortune by Christine Rimmer

Millionaire rancher and eligible bachelor Flynt Carson struck a hole in one when his Sunday golf ritual at the Lone Star Country Club unveiled an abandoned baby girl. Flynt felt he had no business raising a child, and desperately needed the help of former flame Josie Lavender. Though this woman was too innocent for his tarnished soul, the love-struck nanny was determined to help him raise the mysterious baby—and what happened next was anyone's guess!

Available at your favorite retail outlet.

Where love comes alive™

**Where royalty and romance
go hand in hand...**

The series continues in Silhouette Romance
with these unforgettable novels:

HER ROYAL HUSBAND
by Cara Colter
on sale July 2002 (SR #1600)

THE PRINCESS HAS AMNESIA!
by Patricia Thayer
on sale August 2002 (SR #1606)

SEARCHING FOR HER PRINCE
by Karen Rose Smith
on sale September 2002 (SR #1612)

And look for more Crown and Glory stories in
SILHOUETTE DESIRE starting in October 2002!

Available at your favorite retail outlet.

Where love comes alive™

If you enjoyed what you just read,
then we've got an offer you can't resist!

Take 2 bestselling love stories FREE!

Plus get a FREE surprise gift!

Clip this page and mail it to Silhouette Reader Service™

IN U.S.A.	IN CANADA
3010 Walden Ave.	P.O. Box 609
P.O. Box 1867	Fort Erie, Ontario
Buffalo, N.Y. 14240-1867	L2A 5X3

YES! Please send me 2 free Silhouette Desire® novels and my free surprise gift. After receiving them, if I don't wish to receive anymore, I can return the shipping statement marked cancel. If I don't cancel, I will receive 6 brand-new novels every month, before they're available in stores! In the U.S.A., bill me at the bargain price of $3.34 plus 25¢ shipping and handling per book and applicable sales tax, if any*. In Canada, bill me at the bargain price of $3.74 plus 25¢ shipping and handling per book and applicable taxes**. That's the complete price and a savings of at least 10% off the cover prices—what a great deal! I understand that accepting the 2 free books and gift places me under no obligation ever to buy any books. I can always return a shipment and cancel at any time. Even if I never buy another book from Silhouette, the 2 free books and gift are mine to keep forever.

225 SEN DFNS
326 SEN DFNT

Name	(PLEASE PRINT)	
Address	Apt.#	
City	State/Prov.	Zip/Postal Code

* Terms and prices subject to change without notice. Sales tax applicable in N.Y.
** Canadian residents will be charged applicable provincial taxes and GST.
All orders subject to approval. Offer limited to one per household and not valid to current Silhouette Desire® subscribers.
® are registered trademarks of Harlequin Enterprises Limited.

DES01   ©1998 Harlequin Enterprises Limited

COMING NEXT MONTH

SDCNM0602